Mom

Praise for KAYE GIBBONS and
<u>SIGHTS UNSEEN</u>

"Ms. Gibbons has a natural gift for telling stories."
The New York Times

"Wise and rambunctious are the voices of Southern
women, and in Kaye Gibbons's expertly crafted
novels, they sing of love, sustenance and survival."
Miami Herald

"This is Gibbon's best novel since *Ellen Foster*,
a haunting story that begs to be read in one sitting . . .
Readers will be thoroughly in thrall to her clear, true
voice and to the poignant story she tells."
Publishers Weekly

"There is something enduring, genuine,
and original in Kaye Gibbons's work."
Washington Post

"Kaye Gibbons has a voice that will loll comfortably in
a reader's mind long after her tales have been told."
San Diego Union-Tribune

W9-CED-932

Other Avon Books by
Kaye Gibbons

CHARMS FOR THE EASY LIFE

Kaye Gibbons

SIGHTS UNSEEN

AVON BOOKS  NEW YORK

**VISIT OUR WEBSITE AT
http://AvonBooks.com**

AVON BOOKS
A division of
The Hearst Corporation
1350 Avenue of the Americas
New York, New York 10019

Copyright © 1995 by Kaye Gibbons
Published by arrangement with G. P. Putnam's Sons, a Division of the Putnam Berkley Group, Inc.
Library of Congress Catalog Card Number: 95-9781
ISBN: 0-380-72681-5

First Avon Books Printing: November 1996
First Avon Books International Printing: March 1996

AVON TRADEMARK REG. U.S. PAT. OFF. AND IN OTHER COUNTRIES, MARCA REGISTRADA, HECHO EN U.S.A.

Printed in the U.S.A.

RA 10 9 8 7 6 5 4 3 2 1

FOR FRANK

For there are dark streams in this dark world, lady,
Gulf Streams and Arctic currents of the soul.

CONRAD AIKEN, *Preludes for Memnon*

SIGHTS
UNSEEN

I

I

One

Had I known my mother was being given electroconvulsive therapy while I was dressing for school on eight consecutive Monday mornings, I do not think I could have buttoned my blouses or tied my shoes or located my homework. I see myself fumbling with the snap on my skirt, trying to connect the sides, turning around in a circle like a cat chasing its tail. I was twelve, deemed too young to be told what was happening to her and in fact too innocent to surmise it.

There was a certain power in her healing that I, as a child, felt was beyond my capacity to comprehend, the way I, as an adult, cannot comprehend the largeness of the universe, the number of its stars, the heat of the sun, or the speed of light. I could not fathom how such a terribly sick woman could get well. Unless the doctors were using some sort of medical magic, I could not understand how pills and a changed environment were helping when her family's love had been of no use. I believe I was jealous of the hospital and her doctors. At home, she had simply endured her life. In the hospital, she began to flourish. She returned home an independent woman.

I worried about my own lack of influence in her life. If I had a little girl, I thought, I would look at her and discover ways to ground myself. I would find reasons to move out of the haze and into the clearing, where a husband, a son, and a daughter could see me fully and welcome me. If I had a daughter as needy for my love as I was for hers, I could, I thought, will myself to be well for her sake. But Mother did not find that inspiration in me. Her illness, manic depression, was beyond her control. Along with my father, I mourned the inability to change her, to restore her. And I worried that later, when she had been back home with us for a while, the pills and the doctoring would stop working and she would revert to her old crazy ways, and once more, the voices of my father, my brother, and me would be no more than background noise to her ravings. I worried that her wellness would not take, the way vaccinations take. Life with Mother, I feared, would again be life with a stranger, a changeable stranger.

Because of her illness, it was impossible for her to be with us all the time. However, I always maintained the notion that I deserved a mother and would someday have mine. Instead of playing solitaire at the kitchen table while Pearl, our cook and housekeeper, fixed dinner, I would deal a hand of old maid or spades with my mother. She would join me in my life. I hoped for that even in the worst of times. As much as Pearl mothered me, she never let me forget for a minute that I had my own mother upstairs resting or in that hospital, and someday all would be well in our household. I am drawn to know why and how I never abandoned the ideal of a mother. She gave me ample opportunity to ostracize her completely. Why did I "turn out"? Why did my brother "turn out"?

Mother was depressed almost always, and her sadness was fractured only by wild, delusional turns of mind, with brief periods of stability that were celebrated and remembered by my family as though they were spectacular occurrences, like total eclipses or meteor showers. Had she not crashed to a halt in 1967, I would never have known her. I would have been raised wholly by my father and Pearl, and I would have spoiled my life trying to mitigate the ill effects her absence might have forced on me.

A girl cannot go along motherless without life's noticing, taking a compensatory tuck here and there in the heart and in the mind, letting out one seam or another whenever she is threatened by her loneliness. I could have lurched on ahead to adulthood, straining to be a good girl, not ever learning what to do when my own children were placed in my arms. My instinct might have been to ignore my responsibility for them the way my mother had initially relinquished responsibility for me. The children might have had to wait for me to find my way, as I had had to wait for my mother, and they might not have been as patient. My patience came from a deep longing for an ideal, and had I not pitied my mother, I would have stopped waiting for her, given up on her and ranged about for love elsewhere. But we caught each other just in time, right on the edge of my puberty. She pulled me back from the rim of an abyss. Just when I should have been growing away from my mother, we moved toward each other. When I should have been running out of the house with the screen door slamming in my wake, I was crawling into her arms. Boys, when they finally took notice of me, had to wait for my mother and me to learn each other, to learn our habits and our ways.

Mother died five years ago, right after I found out I was pregnant with my first daughter. She was well by then, bolstered by fifteen years of medication and therapy for her manic depression. My brother, Freddy, and I had gone to help her and my father one quiet Sunday afternoon as they cleaned his childhood belongings out of the Barnes family homeplace. My father's father had left the house to his sister-in-law, Miss Josephine Woodward, as a life estate. Although my parents preferred to say that Mr. Barnes and Miss Woodward "kept company," my Aunt Menefee, who was with us that day, said they were "involved." Aunt Menefee's husband, my father's brother, Uncle Lawrence, was with us also, likewise taking his childhood things from the house. Miss Woodward had just gotten out of the hospital after a bout with pneumonia, convinced that in no time she would be sick again and then, shortly, dead. I was to move into the house after her death. My grandfather had bequeathed the house to me as an homage to my mother. I would have let everything stay in the attic. In fact, it would have been soothing to consider my father's childhood toys up there, dusty and untouched for fifty years, but Miss Woodward said she was getting her affairs in order, and that included clearing out and cleaning up her house. My parents, my brother, and I saw no harm in humoring her, but my Aunt Menefee complained as the attic stairs were pulled down. "It's just like her," she said, "to try to dictate to our family. This stuff isn't bothering her. I'm surprised she's not in here orchestrating." I could not imagine Miss Woodward, who was eighty then and asleep in another part of the house, getting out of bed to supervise the removal.

The year was 1982. Mother was sixty-two then, trim as she had always been, except during the times when new medications made her gain weight. I remember how Freddy had commented that day on her size, telling her to wrap her thumb and forefinger around her wrist to prove to herself exactly how skinny she was. She always believed she was fat, and getting fatter. As doctors, Freddy and I believed that Mother needed to eat more, that she took in far more medication and Tab than she did food. Her metabolism seemed to be like that of an eighteen-year-old boy.

The day we emptied the attic, Freddy, my father, and I had told Mother not to lift heavy boxes, and especially not to carry any down those steps. But she did. Her habit of mind made her ignore us all. She came face forward down the stairs, the way she had always taught us never to descend from the attic, holding a box full of my father's old childhood games, lead soldiers, blocks. When she reached the third step from the top, she put one heel on the edge of the step and fell, landing at my father's feet. He had been reprimanding her, but he stopped the instant she tilted off the stairs, like a diver checking the pool beneath her. The contents of the box went sprawling, and then seconds later, without a word or sigh, she died. I have always believed she died in the process of her descent, never comprehending the lightning approach or the eternal finality of her end.

Although this may seem unusual, my first thought at her death was not of my father, or of my brother, or even of her, but of me. I sat down on the floor by her, wondering how I could carry my baby the distance of seven months and my lifetime without her. And I believed that I had earned the right, as a small child in our turbulent home, to mourn for myself first.

Miss Woodward came toddling down the hall from her room and saw us all there, still and staring at my mother. "Why, pray tell, don't you call the ambulance?" she asked. My father, my brother, Uncle Lawrence, Aunt Menefee, and I looked at one another as if to acknowledge that this was indeed a fair question. We were just so stunned, you see. My mother's death defied us all. She was not, nor had she ever been, the kind of woman who would die without some quality of drama, a drawn-out illness that would require her to give directions from a hospital bed while wearing a silk quilted bed jacket and two coats of frosted lipstick. Earlier in her life, she was the kind of woman who would have killed herself, but when she became well, she developed an abundance of pride. Very simply, my mother endured so much in her time that she was proud to be alive.

I wonder at her short fall from the attic stairs. I wonder whether she looked at me and thought, Hattie, I will never see your baby. Or whether she looked at my brother and remembered the distance between them as he was growing up. Did she recall his marathons of avoiding her, of walking out of rooms she entered? And my father! Did she look at him and say in silence, "You know I have always loved you, Frederick. Even before you were born." I hope she had time to consider us all as we considered her on her tumble down and caught our breath in the instant. At the funeral home the next evening, my father said, "I thought Maggie was only falling. I thought I would help her to her feet and tell her not to go up those damn steps again and then stand there watching her while she did that very thing."

"I know," I told him. "I know."

Although she was sixty-two, she had not lived as a whole, rounded person but fifteen years. Before, as I have said, she rotated in and out of wellness. In 1967, when I was twelve, her doctor pieced together a narrative of her life to that point and calculated that she had experienced no fewer than twenty complete cycles of mania and depression. But 1967 was the year life changed for her, the autumn of her crisis and her homecoming. She had enjoyed sound reason for close to twelve months, and then, late one Saturday morning, after a few weeks' prelude of ascension that was beyond my father's ability to control, she sneaked downstairs and stole the car keys from the ring by the back door. We did not know she was gone until it was too late. We thought she was reading and listening to the radio in her room, where Father had left her after having sat up all night listening to her chatter about one thing and the next. Father had convinced her that, because of her illness, having a driver's license would not be a wise idea for her, but she navigated the seven miles from Bend of the River Road to Rocky Mount and, proceeding down a cobbled side street that was made not for vehicles, but only for pedestrians, bumped a woman with the car. By the time Mother hit her, the muffler and oil pan of the Oldsmobile were dragging on the cobblestones, so noisily that curious shopkeepers rushed to their front doors. The policemen were able to file such a full report because people were eager to talk about what they had just witnessed. My mother talked, too. She told the arresting officer what she fully perceived to be the truth: She was on her way to the shoe store because the radio announcer had told her to come downtown right away, and then she saw this woman on the sidewalk wearing her clothes, trying to look just like her, and she despised it when people tried to mimic her, and she thought she would just knock the woman with the car and teach her a lesson and see if she came downtown dressed in clothes that she had no business wearing because only Maggie Barnes wore a red swing coat with a black collar and if somebody had to be arrested then what about locking up that bitch who was in there sniveling about her bruised, fat hips that could stand a clip off either side anyway.

Mother was coherent enough to demand that someone call my father. He could not be reached, because he had left for the fields, so she had the policeman's partner call her father-in-law, Mr. Barnes. Looking back, I see that he was a more logical choice anyway. He knew how to take matters in hand better than my father. Mr. Barnes was a fixer. Mother was in deep trouble and needed someone who could act with great exactitude and certainty. Had Mr. Barnes not appeared shortly, Mother might have been locked up still ranting about her broad-beamed tormentor. He parked his car and walked down the cobblestone street, to find Mother behind the wheel of the Oldsmobile, screaming at the policemen through her open window. Seeing her, as I can now, through the eyes of onlookers, I am embarrassed for her. I want to turn back the clock and be there beside her in the car with the courage to tell curiosity-seekers to back away.

Mr. Barnes offered the policemen some money and came dangerously close to being arrested for bribery, although he did manage to persuade the officers to let him drive Mother to the magistrate's office. And so he put her in the backseat of his car, and off they went across town, with Mother simultaneously huffy and wild. She was released into his custody. Then, realizing that a news story would humiliate my mother once she was well enough to know what she had done, Mr. Barnes drove to the *Evening Telegram* office, where he flashed the same bills the policemen had earlier rejected.

Mr. Barnes must have been able to persuade someone at the newspaper to accept those bills, because he succeeded in having my mother's manic tale edited; but edited, my mother sounds disorganized and mean-spirited. The story lacks the high velocity and fluidity with which, when on a roll, she could glide from one topic to the next, from the poisoning of the American mind by Ed Sullivan, to the moral superiority of *Dragnet*'s Joe Friday, to the Yankee conspiracy to dismantle Southern values by introducing hard rolls into the bread section of the Colonial Store. When almost at the height of a manic episode, as a last blowout she could deliver dinner-table filibusters that either made all the sense in the world or made none at all, and after listening to her for an hour or so, nobody could tell the difference. The report makes my mother say she ran the woman down because she had fat hips, when what Mother had really meant was that the woman, by her dress and haughty gait, was trying to steal her soul. When she was sick, the theft of her soul by strangers was a topic she dwelt upon. Long after she recovered, she said she had been afraid of being left a shell of a person, a husk.

Between my parents' 1947 wedding and early 1954, Mother's rotations of mood had caused five maids to quit, and then finally my father found Pearl Wiggins, who could ride out my mother's storms better than anyone, including Mr. Barnes. My mother's illness did not addle Pearl, who knew how to maintain the distance necessary to avoid being drawn into its vortex. She had stamina and could plow her feet forward and stop a rebuke on a dime, if necessary, to avoid losing patience with Mother. Pearl always believed that her loss of patience would be the first step in letting Mother's illness creep up on her. "If I had gotten mad with her, I could have become befuddled, and that would have been the last of me," she once told me.

Although Pearl could be firm with Mother, sometimes Mother did need to be coaxed. I can remember one time when I was six, following Mother's screams downstairs to the kitchen to find her arm up and back like a pitcher's, coffee cup in hand. She yelled, "I'll break the goddamn thing right now! Leave me alone!"

Pearl approached her as though she were walking toward a madman with a loaded gun, and said, "Give me the cup, Miss Maggie. You break that and you'll break up your whole set of blue-and-white. Once you straighten out, you'll hate yourself and me, too, for letting you to do it."

I watched from the steps that led into the kitchen by the stove. Mother seemed to regain her composure long enough to know that she did not want to break a cup that had belonged to her grandmother. So she gave it to Pearl. Then she sat down at the table and cried. She said she had no idea why she was so mad.

"I don't know, either," Pearl told her. "You just sit there and let me peel you an orange."

Pearl did this, and then she saw me and invited me in to sit at the table and share the orange with Mother. I, frankly, was afraid to eat the woman's orange. It seemed to be all she had in the world right then. She devoured it without acknowledging my presence at the table. Afterward, Pearl called Mother to the sink, where she washed her hair. Because of her illness, Mother did not get out to the beauty shop. Pearl, who often brought the conveniences of the outside world into our house, rolled Mother's hair, set her under the dome dryer that was kept in the laundry room, and handed her a movie magazine.

On so many days Pearl had to regard my mother as a hospital nurse would a stubborn invalid who clamps her mouth shut at feeding time. She attributed her ability to handle Mother mainly to her experience serving as live-in companion to a person she called "the eyebrow woman" in Raleigh before World War II. This woman suffered from a condition that compelled her to tweeze her eyebrows and other hairs she found on her body, and Pearl felt that if she could manage someone with this phenomenal compulsion, she could manage my mother. She told my father that she had learned how to run a household with a "rickety woman" in the place.

She said, "You do what needs to be done when it needs doing, just like in a regular house, except you have to keep your eye on the sick one the way you do a mean child. You can't let either one have a pair of scissors or a box of matches."

The first direction Mother went in after Pearl arrived was down. Father has said that she was in rare form for Freddy's sixth birthday, soon after she became pregnant with me. The noise coming up the stairwell and through the heating vents from the dining room to her bedroom was amplified by what Father always called her strong urge for the silence of the tomb. She yelled that she wanted to shut her eyes in peace.

"All I want to do is sleep! Can't you hear me down there? Please, for God's sake, be quiet!" Pearl said my mother screamed herself hoarse. Then, when my brother scraped the bottom of an ice cream dish with a spoon, she appeared downstairs in the dining room, looking as though she actually had not slept at all in the weeks she swore it had been since she had had any peace. She demanded to know who was scraping the bowl. Everyone was intent on driving her mad, she declared. If she could just get some rest, fourteen or fifteen hours of undisturbed sleep, maybe she would feel human. But no. Somebody had to scrape the last bit of ice cream out of the goddamn bowl. "Why don't you lick it?" she shouted.

My father promised that he and Pearl would keep everything calm, and then Mr. Barnes volunteered to walk Mother back upstairs. Freddy hissed something nasty about her spoiling his party, which was not a bona fide party anyway because no friends were there to share his cake with him. Just my father, and Aunt Menefee's seven-year-old son, Marshall, his five- and six-year-old sisters, Ruth and Carol, and Pearl and Mr. Barnes were there to help him celebrate. Outsiders could enter the house only while Mother was well, but they were so unaccustomed to coming that we seldom had visitors. So much happened in our house that was never to be seen. If children, besides Aunt Menefee's, had come to play with Freddy when Mother was either up or down, and then had gone home to report what they had seen, that would have been their last trip to the Barnes house. She could have wilted a bunch of children standing around the dining room table, wearing pointed hats, blowing paper horns. If the sound of a spoon on a bowl was intolerable, she could not have borne whoops and toots.

After Mr. Barnes settled her in bed, he came back downstairs, jerked Freddy up to his room, and yelled him into admitting that he was a rude little bastard. Then he commanded

Freddy to go apologize to Mother. He gave him the language, which Freddy told me he never forgot: "Apologize as if you mean it. Tell her you are sorry for the disrespect, and that it will never happen again. She's in there crying her heart out. Can you hear it? Hear it? You caused it. Shuffling your feet and moaning 'Sorry' would be more cruel than simply ignoring her entirely." That was only one of Freddy's first memories of our grandfather. I was to learn early on that Freddy was the easy brunt of Mr. Barnes's discontent with himself and the world, and so I also learned, in self-defense, to do no wrong in his eyes.

Two

Mother's manic episode in 1967 lasted only six weeks, but what a six weeks it was! She swung back and forth between cataclysms of torment and heights of ecstasy. She began by obsessing about television characters. Dr. Bob Hughes and his wife, Kim, from *As the World Turns*, for example, wanted to meet her. She thought she could take Bob away from Kim, who was a weakling. Nice Kim. Well, nice Kim could watch her man being snatched. Bob would be drawn to Mother. Kim took a week deciding whether she wanted to work in the hospital canteen so she could be closer to Bob. She should have taken the job, but no, she vacillated and somebody else took it. Now, there was her attractive husband, roaming the hospital, feeling my mother's power. It would be soon. Soon Bob and Kim would come for dinner, and Bob would kiss Mother's hand upon entering the door and then gaze at her across the table.

My mother, during these six weeks, told my father that he would just have to understand that she had been put on the planet to be worshipped by all men. He could not complain; he knew she was unique when he married her. Men she saw on television or in the movies, and authors of books felt her spirit: David Niven, Anthony Quinn, Maximilian Schell, John Steinbeck, Harold Robbins, Leon Uris, Irving Stone, Richard Burton, Chet Huntley, and David Brinkley. She had a special feeling in her heart, she said, for Robert Kennedy, and he had one for her. Like Bob Hughes, Robert Kennedy would soon arrive for dinner. What did Catholics eat? One day, she bothered Pearl about it, making her look through the indexes of our recipe books for the heading "Catholic." She called the butcher at the Colonial Store and asked him what Catholics who shopped at his store ate. He said that he thought the Doyles were his only Catholic customers, and she told him never mind and called the Doyles directly. Mother sat on the kitchen floor with the telephone in her lap and the cookbooks strewn around her, carrying on a strange, one-sided conversation.

"This is Mrs. Frederick Barnes, and I'm having a Catholic over to dinner, and I understand you're Catholic, and since you are, you might be able to tell me what I ought to feed one. It must be like with the Jews. You can't eat anything you please anytime you like."

Mother bit her nails and listened.

"You said fish? Fish on Friday. I should've known it. So I'm safe with fish. Right?"

Mrs. Doyle, who was probably stunned to have been interrupted by such an odd question, must have assured my mother that fish was the only answer, because when Mother hung up the phone, she said, "Fish, Pearl. Feed him fish. It must have something to do with Jesus and the loaves. I'll have fish sent from the beach. I'll be damned if I'll feed him anything out of the pond. Thank God for flounder."

So Robert Kennedy would be fed fresh flounder. Something would have to be done about Ethel, though. And all those children. Rich children they were, but children all the same. Ethel must have full custody. Robert could move in and conduct his important affairs from our home. Mother would install him at our roll-top mahogany desk with a hot line to Washington. He could bring a secretary. She could have a card table. But that was it. No Ethel. And definitely no children.

My mother was undaunted by the fact that neither Bob Hughes, nor Robert Kennedy, nor Anthony Quinn, nor Harold Robbins appeared at our door. She would bide her time with Father. He was a handsome man, square-shouldered, square-jawed, with black hair salted at the temples with gray. Years of sun had given him a perpetual farmer's tan. His eyes were blue, flecked with green. Maybe Mother had those other men on her mind when she shanghaied my father morning after morning within those six weeks, forcing him to put a latch on their bedroom door.

My father's desire to help Mother find some peace in her life had led to my conception. I was an experimental baby. In 1954, the year of my conception, Father decided that a baby would make my mother feel better. My brother was already past the point of needing mothering of a babyish sort. An infant, Father thought, would give her something to think about, a goal and a purpose to her days. He missed most of her first pregnancy because he was on occupation duty in Japan, but, he once told me, he was encouraged by the memory that she had been stable while Freddy was a tiny baby. Now, with her second pregnancy, he was merely trying to duplicate the experience for her. He persuaded her that being pregnant and then having a cute baby in her arms would make her engine slip into a steady, forward-moving gear.

Pearl believed the opposite. She told my father that another baby would drive my mother into a full-blown, full-time dementia. In my mother's case, two babies was two too many, yet Pearl had relatives in Jonesboro who had more children than they could care for only after the seventh or eighth. They would make fast plans to skim the top off the household by sending away as many servant-age children as they could. Two months before my birth, Pearl's sister decided that one of her middle girls was more of a food intake than a help, and she wrote Pearl to ask if our house was in need of any extra hands. Pearl wrote her back immediately and signed up for one fourteen-year-old girl, Olive, who crammed all her clothes and a tattered stuffed dog into a cardboard suitcase. Everything was figured out and done, Pearl told Father. She announced, as she put on her hat and drove to the bus

station for her niece, that she had even negotiated a salary. He must have blinked at all this
zinging past him. After she left, he said, he
considered how much more work there would
be with a new baby, and he was grateful that
Pearl took the initiative, or at least that she
reached out and caught the help that was
tossed the fifty miles from Jonesboro.

Pearl told me that Mother's behavior while
she was carrying was always peculiar. After
she had started showing with me she went to
a cousin's evening wedding and made a display of herself. She was wearing a long maternity dress of her own design, and when the
church felt a bit too cool for her, she sat up
and pulled the skirt of the dress from underneath her and wrapped it about her shoulders,
like a shawl.

"Your mother," Pearl said, "leaned forward
to grab a hymnal, and everybody on the front
row of the colored balcony could see the entire
back of her slip all the way to her girdle,
which she squoze herself into until the day she
popped the elastic."

Also, Mother seemed to forget at times that
a baby was on the way. Pearl would find her
on the top rung of the step stool, reaching for
high places in the back of her closet. Pearl
would say she should get down before I was

lost or damaged, and my mother would respond, "Oh, okay," as if Pearl had told her the hat she was looking for was in the guest room closet instead of her own. She thought nothing of saddling her horse, of riding her wobbly Schwinn down the sandy mile-long path to Mr. Barnes's house, of taking long hot baths while Pearl stood in the door with a towel, begging her to get out before she gave the baby a soapy-water infection. When, during her eighth month, she went to the state fair with my father and brother and Pearl, she implored the ticket-taker to let her ride the Twister. Neither he nor my father would allow it, so she stood off to the side with Pearl and watched my brother and father swirling about. She cried, and Pearl bought her a cinnamon-coated elephant ear.

When she finally understood the matter, she became convinced that I would be stillborn, and refused to attend a baby shower to be given in her honor. Aunt Menefee had one at her home anyway, without my mother, because minding Mother's business when she believed her to be incapacitated by insanity was such a part of her nature. And because Aunt Menefee's character was basically insipid, according to my father's perceptions when I was a child and my own as an adult when I could see her clearly, she took Mother's refusal to be showered at a little Sunday-afternoon party as a personal affront.

Aunt Menefee invited everybody in the Bend of the River community she thought would come, from the woman who was conceited because she had been to New York, to the elderly elementary school teacher who wore men's hats, to the Britt twins, who were distinguished one from the other by their nicknames, Miss Sewing Britt and Miss Cooking Britt. All her invitations were accepted, probably because people were fascinated with my mother's mysterious mental condition. Women in the community often treated Maggie Barnes as though she were a spectacle, a wonder on the order of the Spaghetti Man, the Italian corpse that lay unclaimed and glass-encased for viewing in a Laurinburg funeral parlor. Aunt Menefee probably remarked, at different times, that any number of these women were her best friends in the whole wide world, but my mother could not say that. She had only Pearl, my father, and his father for good friends. Aunt Menefee was in the middle of everything, comprehending little about Mother's illness or about why she could never appear at socials, sewing circles, barbecues, and quiltings. Pearl said that Aunt Menefee would often ask if Maggie had the blahs again. She did not understand that a trip to town for a manicure would not pull Mother out of the doldrums if she was too low, or that a nice vacation to somewhere like the Grove Park Inn would not ease her spirit if she was too high.

Days before I was born, there was no room made up for me in the house. Freddy hounded Pearl to fix some sort of space for me, as he worried about being ousted from his room. She assured him that by the time I came home from the hospital, the spare bedroom would be covered with baby paraphernalia.

The morning Father took Mother to the hospital, he left a great deal of hustling about in the charge of Pearl, who, with Hubert, the combination handyman, yardman, and driver, who reported to her and had worked at our house since Freddy was a baby, took the convertible bathtub-and-changing-table that Pearl had borrowed from Aunt Menefee out of its storage place in a shed, and assembled a crib that had been stored in the basement. Pearl had already stockpiled diapers, plastic pants, a Bambi mobile, little smocked gowns, drawstring sleepers, rattles, and all the other shower gifts. Out everything came, from boxes and bags, the basement, the attic, closets. Pearl said the house was like midnight on a Christmas Eve, except my father was not frantically putting a bicycle together. By the time I was born, I had something of a conventional nursery.

When my schedule caused me difficulties in nursing my second daughter, my father told me that Mother had had so little milk to offer that the maternity staff at the hospital supplemented her thin and inconsequential drips with a formula of sugar and evaporated milk, which I enjoyed so much that on the third day after my birth I would tolerate nothing else. She cursed the nurses, calling them kidnappers, strumpets, and whores, and said she would throw herself through the window if I was not brought to her for my next feeding, before they alienated me further with another bottle. They consented, and so she opened her nightgown, lay on her side, and let the nurse arrange my body at her breast. Father said that I rooted around, attached my mouth to her, and then wailed after I sucked furiously, sensing that I would parch if I kept this up much longer. My bleary newborn eyes must have crossed in ecstasy when the nurse took me back to the nursery and stuck a bottle in my mouth. Mother told the staff that I was not to be brought to her for the duration of our stay, and then she told Father that they would collect me on her way home, as if I were an overcoat or an umbrella that she had checked. If I did not need her, she cried, she did not need me. Father told me he could not make her understand that I did not know what or whom I needed. He said she would not listen when he said that I just wanted to fill my stomach. That explanation of my frustration at her breast was not good enough. She thought she saw a sign.

My rejection of her, she told Father, was a precursor of our future relationship, and she actually asked him if they could try for another baby, one who might like her. My Aunt Menefee could take me. Mother's maternal instincts were jammed at a time when they should have been surging.

In front of my father, the woman she shared the room with insulted her by saying things like, "You need a calm frame of mind to nurse a baby," and "As a rule, a hysterical woman cannot nurse, and you, missy, are a mess. No wonder you can't let down. Try to feed a baby that way and see if she doesn't get a case of nerves." She told my father he should ask the nurses to give Mother something to knock her out or at least to subdue her. The woman said she had four children, and she had nursed them all until they cut teeth and bit her. She let my mother know time and time again the relationship between a mother's mood and her ability to nurse a baby. This woman was like a chorus, all the various voices from my mother's life now in unison, telling her how much joy she could have if she were normal, happy, and sane.

When the woman from the medical records office came around for my mother to sign my birth certificate, my mother told her I was to be named Harriet and be called Hattie. The woman whispered in Mother's ear.

"Mrs. Barnes," she said, "you can't call her Hattie. Hattie's a little nigger name."

Mother commanded the woman to write down "Harriet," a name my father had chosen, and also to list my middle name as Pearl. The woman suggested other names that were popular then, such as Susan and Karen and Elizabeth. My mother told her "Harriet Pearl" would be adequate, and after she signed the certificate, she turned over and sobbed into her pillow. When she spoke, it was only to beg her roommate to tell her if she thought she had given her baby an ugly name, if the name did indeed sound too colored. She hounded this woman, asking again and again, "Oh God, what have I done?" until the woman asked to be transferred to another room. No other patient was given her bed. My mother lay there alone, crying over her ambivalent feelings toward my name.

My name was that of my father's mother, who had dropped dead in the business office of this same hospital while my grandfather was settling her bill. She was thought to have been cured of phlebitis, but a blood clot traveled to her heart and surprised them all as she stood quietly by her husband, waiting to go home and make fig preserves and tend to her flock of unruly peacocks. For a coming-home present, Mr. Barnes had in his car a fresh case of mason jars. He left the jars in the parking lot at the hospital, and told his sons that same afternoon that he would not have a bunch of disappointed jars in his house. As much as my grandfather cherished my mother, he invented a range of reasons why he could not visit her or the new baby in this hospital. Suddenly, the highway into town was a racetrack, a goddamn racetrack, he was apt to say, and he was not about to get on it. And his eyes had started bothering him, blurring when he met streams of oncoming traffic.

Nobody urged Mr. Barnes to endure his sorrow long enough to visit, because nobody urged Mr. Barnes to do anything. Nobody reminded him that he drove all over the county checking on his various properties every day and that he took this same highway whenever he attended a Junior Order meeting or followed a load of tobacco to market. Reminding him of these things was simply not done, just as calling him Grandfather was not done. He was called Mr. Barnes by anyone who was not in the position to call him Father. He bristled at familiarity and spurned his grandchildren's hopes for intimacy. Once, when Marshall was four, he mounted Mr. Barnes's crossed leg as he sat on the tailgate of a truck with some other men, probably discussing things like the high cost of hail insurance, or the low prices of hogs and cattle. Marshall meant to ride the little horse to town, but Mr. Barnes said, "Get off me," and angled his foot, causing my cousin to slip to the ground and lose his wind. Mr. Barnes's friends laughed at Marshall's audacity and teased him about joining the rodeo circuit.

Three

Ordinarily, Father was up at dawn, out the door and working for Mr. Barnes long before I caught the school bus. But in that period before Mother bumped the woman, when she was substituting him for actors, writers, and politicians, she nearly killed him. Sometimes I would come off the bus in the afternoons to find him adrift in the house in khaki pants and a rumpled undershirt, looking like a hall-walker in a veterans' hospital, spent and forlorn. I remember wondering if he had the flu or mononucleosis, an illness that had kept a friend of mine out of school for a month. Ironically, I realized later, he did have a ''kissing disease." One Saturday morning as I walked past the closed door to my parents' bedroom, I found out why he had been sighing and dragging himself through the house.

Mother was growling at him about his wanting to leave the room. "You've got to finish what you've started," she said.

"But it'll take all day, Maggie. I have to get some work done."

"To hell with work. Come here."

I stood there listening, and I heard them moaning as though they were both tied to a rack of some sort and struggling to break free. There was an urgency and depth to their voices that I had never heard before, not even from Mother, who, because of her illness, had a wide range of sounds, from raucous laughter to a raw, throaty roar. Pearl, who was walking up the kitchen stairs with the vacuum cleaner, saw me and motioned me toward her. She propped the vacuum cleaner against the wall on the landing and pointed for me to go downstairs. She followed me. When we reached the kitchen, she told me she would go ahead and make that evening's bread and then vacuum later. I wanted to be upstairs, but she would not let me.

Sitting at the kitchen table, I wondered at the moaning while Pearl made a big racket accumulating the supplies to make bread. She sang a loud, rather mumbling and tuneless song about Jesus. But still, she could not drown out the sounds from overhead. I told her I needed to get a schoolbook from my room, and she told me I could wait until later. She said I was not going upstairs until she had given me permission. She kept me occupied, as she sometimes did, by giving me a mound of bread dough to knead into my own miniature loaf. I noticed that she kept glancing up at the ceiling as she punched and turned her dough. I asked if my parents were all right.

"She is. He's not," Pearl answered.

"What's wrong with Father?"

"Nothing her keeping her hands to her sides won't cure."

That day, Pearl told me the story of how she came to work for my family. She talked loud to compete with Mother's noise, and the fat under her arms dangled and jiggled as she punched and kneaded the dough.

She said, "I was working for a no-count man in Sharpsburg, you see, and one night at Renfrow's Broasted Chicken I heard about how your daddy couldn't keep help. Two ladies that had tried working here were sitting at my table. They told me about your mother. They said she slept all the time or wouldn't sleep, and she hopped on their backs and stayed on them until the day they had their fill and walked out the door. I says, 'That woman will be no problem to me!' They said, 'You try her, then!' So I did. I came to the door, that door right there, and saw your mother through the screen. She was at the stove cooking everything there was in the house. I says, 'That woman is not right.' I could tell by looking at her. She was just jerking. I came on in the house without a knock and put my hands on hers while she was slicing vegetables all over her nice countertop. Just ruining it. She stopped, put the knife down, and sat in the chair I pulled out for her. She had never laid eyes on me, but she trusted me. You see? Then your daddy came downstairs. I gave her the newspaper and said, 'Now, you look at the pictures, Mrs. Barnes, while I talk to your husband.' Then she started to cry that she was no good.

" 'Yes, you are good,' I told her. 'You've got a nice pot of something on the boil. You've been very busy! Yes, you are some good!'

"She looked at the pictures like she was told to do while I spoke with your father. He didn't even ask who I was. He acted like I was an employment gift from God. I introduced myself, and then he told me I ought not to have gotten that close to Miss Maggie, she with a knife in her hand. I told him I would be moving into a room up the stairs, one near hers, and I would cook, as soon as Miss Maggie's creation was eaten, if it was eatable at all, and I would clean top to bottom, do laundry, iron, sew, shop, and entertain that little boy who came running in the door and interrupted me talking. I said I would keep your mother from hurting herself or anybody else when she was ill. I said I would also require a dependable automobile. That was a lot of saying, but he listened and took it all in. I could see he was a smart man, worked to death, though, and ground-down worried over his wife.

" 'I'll not drive the automobile you use to haul field hands around in,' I told him. I said I wanted something respectable, and if he lacked the means to buy it, I would drive his car till he found them. I said I wanted twenty dollars a week, knowing myself that other women were making ten.

" 'Think how much it'll be worth,' I told him, 'to go to work and not look up and see black smoke and wonder if that's Mrs. Barnes burning the house down.' "

Just when Pearl had talked herself out, when this installment of how she came to be with us was over, Mother finally allowed Fa-

ther to leave their room. He came downstairs
into the kitchen and told Pearl to phone Miss
Woodward, who was sympathetic to his plight
over Mother's illness, and say he was on his
way over. He was going there to take a nap.
He would not have gone to his father's because he could not have confided in him without hearing about how he did not know how
to look after my mother. And probably he
chose not to go to his brother's because of the
houseful of rambunctious children over there.
He was using Miss Woodward's tidy little
mansard-roofed bungalow as a refuge from
Mother's rampage. Now I see that he was hiding from sex, although I doubt that he told
Miss Woodward exactly why he needed to be
there. He would not have considered it
something he could tell a woman, no matter
how close to the family she was. He probably
set up the guest bedroom arrangement with
her by saying he needed somewhere to take a
rest from Mother's illness, and that was all.
She was not the kind of woman who would
have burdened him with questions. She was
always ready to accommodate both my father
and Uncle Lawrence, whose periodic fights
with Aunt Menefee drove him from his own
house.

I imagined Father in her spare bedroom,

which I had once peeked into, sleeping on a twin bed, covered by a white chenille spread. I imagined he was as far underneath the covers as he could go. He probably wanted to disappear, to heal himself in slumber, I thought. I remember that Pearl, after a while, phoned to see how he was doing and was told he was awake but did not want to come home until he knew Mother was asleep. An hour or so later, Pearl phoned back and assured Father he was safe. He slid through the doorway, Pearl said, like a thief in his own house.

When I eventually understood what had happened to Father, I was at first repulsed by the sheer crudeness of the act; then, by the time I was married and knew about sex well enough for myself, I was amazed at what a dynamo my mother had been. Except when she was sick, her emotions were well contained. She wore white gloves to church and crossed her feet at the ankles. She could have passed for a finishing-school graduate. But that was in her brief intervals of sanity. Otherwise, she could be wild. I imagined her reclined on her bed, dressed in a negligee, hooking her forefinger toward my father as he begged for a little respite. I imagined that he relented because she was too strong to be resisted. I assumed her loveliness weakened his

41

resolve. And I suppose I was envious of their intimacy. She and I had nothing to compare with her relationship with my father. They were one unit, and my brother and I were adjuncts. She rarely touched us, except to run her fingers absentmindedly through our hair when she was near us, talking to somebody else, such as our father or Mr. Barnes.

Four

Mr. Barnes was a man of means, a rural capitalist. He owned five hundred acres of land, and rumors on Bend of the River Road had him endowed with a quarter-million dollars in People's Bank. Although it was never discussed in the family, he was the absentee landlord of a disreputable pool hall that had always been phenomenally profitable because of the every-day-and-especially-on-Sunday sale of bootleg whiskey out the back door. During the postwar building boom, he divided profits from the sale of tremendous stands of walnut trees between his two sons. He sold the land upon which a regional airport was later built, and he also negotiated access across his land to the county's new reservoir. He always seemed to have the right real estate at the right time. The Barneses might have been the only farming family in the eastern part of North Carolina to dread the day that someone might have to dip into capital.

My father was a gentleman farmer. Had we lived in town, my family would have owned the hardware store, the drugstore, the car dealership, an apartment building or two, and possibly a small department store. Had this been the mid-nineteenth century instead of the twentieth, our farm would have been called a plantation; the house, the Big House; the tenant farmers, slaves; and my mother, a classic nervous matriarch who suffered spells.

Mr. Barnes had a dark view of the capabilities of his two sons, my father and Uncle Lawrence, treating them as though they were slackers and shirkers who needed to be continually whipped to the front lines. When they spoke, to inform him of some event on the farm, for example, he always responded as if they were lying. He wanted proof that the barn of tobacco was sold at a particular price, proof that corn needed irrigating or that certain alcoholic employees were unavailable because they were laid up in town on a Monday morning.

My father's slight limp, which always made him look as though he was enduring a bunion or a plantar wart, was prompted by his fear of his father. At twelve, he rode a mare that had not been broken, one he had been warned not to go near. When he fell and cracked his ankle, he was afraid to tell his father and did not see a doctor. Uncle Lawrence, who was a year older than my father, set the ankle and bound it with wood and rawhide. Father laced his foot up in tight leather brogans and worked for the next two months at not hobbling in his father's presence. When he was found out, when he finally had to tell his father why he was limping, he was taken to a doctor's office, where the ankle was reset and wrapped in plaster. Later, at home, Father was beaten about the legs with a razor strop.

When Uncle Lawrence spilled India ink on his bedsheets while playing with his cartoon kit, he gave the laundress fifty cents to make the sheets disappear and replace them with clean ones without a word to his father. Neither my father nor Uncle Lawrence could have confided in their mother, because she had no secrets from her husband, having relinquished her authority over the children to him as soon as they were out of diapers. My father once told me that they were never sure how much they could trust her with news of themselves, their crushes, their schoolyard fights, and the like, because she was a conduit to their father. They treated her with tender respect, and held their secrets for the laundress and each other.

When his two sons married, Mr. Barnes built them replicas of his own house, only smaller. He even installed a formal garden with a trellised entry on the side of each house, with bulbs and cuttings from my grandmother's very large garden. He planned the houses with a main entrance into a rarely used formal room. Everybody came and went through the back door, which opened onto a wide porch with Florida windows. Three metal gliders with green cotton pillows lined the porch at our house. My father sometimes napped on one of these after lunch, usually for no more than ten or fifteen minutes, for Mr. Barnes would expect him back at work. Off the porch was the kitchen, by far the biggest room in the house. We had a brick oven in addition to our regular one, just as Mr. Barnes had in his house. The only variation in our house was the interior decoration, which my mother decided would be Early American. She systematically decorated the house until it was bulging. Mr. Barnes's house was full of Victorian furniture that had come down from Virginia with my grandmother's family. He saw that it was cleaned and oiled twice a year. He despised having children put their fingers on anything.

On Christmas Eve of 1941, when Mother was twenty-one, my father proposed to her. He had just enlisted in the Army. They decided to become engaged, wait out the war, and then marry. She once told me that she did not want to think of herself forever as a war bride, to believe that desperation or urgency had anything to do with her decision. Mother must have been completely well at the time. Had she been manic, she would have been incapable of delaying the wedding. Had she been depressed, she would have been incapable of accepting my father. He saw no danger of her getting away from him. He trusted her. Only in her dreams or on a manic tear would she ever have imagined herself with anyone other than my father. Because they had been friends all their lives and because Father was extraordinarily patient with her flighty nature, the match, they both told me, seemed especially propitious.

Since high school, Mother had been working

at an insurance agency in Nashville, the
county seat. She was stable enough to work
regularly, although depression was already
starting to nag her. She would come home
from work, eat, and go to bed thinking her
lethargy was a result of fatigue. Until he went
to training camp, Father saw her on weekends,
and many times he would sit with her in her
parents' living room and watch her dozing on
the sofa.

Mr. Barnes was always there to edge the relationship along if it started to flag. While Father was away, he visited Mother, stopping by
the insurance agency every Friday to take her
to lunch. I think he saw in my mother what
he did not see in his own wife: a sense of adventure in an otherwise ordinary rural life, a
state of being that bordered on danger. My
mother frequently had to be pulled back from
the brink of emotional catastrophe. There was
always something to do where she was concerned. Mr. Barnes's wife required no main-
tenance, while my mother was a challenge. On
her most normal days, she was still more in-
teresting to him than were any of his neighbors. Unlike everybody else in the community,
she dared to talk to Mr. Barnes as though she
were his equal, and it took something akin to
art for my father and him to manage her on a

daily basis. I think Mr. Barnes enjoyed the challenge the way he enjoyed all-night poker games in that pool hall he owned. He embraced her.

Yet I do not think she could have been made to marry my father had she not wanted to. A girl who could drink five highballs and still discreetly lead my father through a perfect jitterbug was not the sort of girl to be pushed into matrimony. And I like to think that she and my father would have eloped if Mr. Barnes had not approved of the union. But there would have been that question of what my father would do for a living. He was wholly dependent on Mr. Barnes for his livelihood. My mother's parents considered the marriage to be what would now be called upwardly mobile. With Mr. Barnes's land and his fortune, they would not have to fret over the responsibility for their daughter. She would be more than well tended to. They both died during my parents' second year of marriage, when another driver crossed a median and met their car head-on. My father told me that Mother sank into a despondency that did not abate for months.

He said that it was actually during the first year of their marriage that Mother's illness started to show itself. One autumn morning, he said, he caught her on her knees at the base of a pine tree in the front yard, arranging the needles in a neat circle. I have always wondered whether she cried when the wind blew. Father led her back into the house, and from that moment on, he was her keeper.

Uncle Lawrence and Aunt Menefee, however, married because of the exigent but uncreative—except in the strictest sense of the word—condition of pregnancy. My cousin Marshall was a counting-fingers baby, the local term for a child born a tad early. Aunt Menefee was not silent in her belief that Mr. Barnes coddled my mother, routinely taking care of her bank overdrafts and charge-a-plate bills. Although my aunt never said anything directly, she remarked constantly that her little family was not a drain on Mr. Barnes, who discounted everything she said or ignored her completely when my mother was around. It was not that Aunt Menefee was physically unattractive or intolerably whiny and petulant, like the pregnant sister in *Cat on a Hot Tin Roof*, who had her own Maggie to deal with. She was simply ordinary, with tendencies toward shrewishness. But Mr. Barnes and my mother operated in the glow of special privilege, he because of his dictatorial nature and she because of the vicissitudes of her illness. Mr.

Barnes's favorite expression was "Aye God."
He was apt to say things such as "Aye God,
I'll be damned if I don't despise a fly." And
so many times I heard him say, "Aye God,
Maggie, don't you look pretty today?" She
would all but twirl for him.

After Mother hit the woman with her car,
the magistrate released her into Mr. Barnes's
custody, and he brought her to our house,
having called Pearl to tell her to get ready.
Freddy went out to the fields and found Father, and he was waiting for her at the door. I
felt as though a circus animal, a tiger or a lion,
was about to be delivered and all the handlers
needed to be on guard with their whips and
chairs. Father had to pull her to their bedroom
by both arms, and she kicked his shins all up
the stairs and through the hall, with Mr.
Barnes walking behind them, in case she
turned and tried to bolt. I followed them at a
safe distance. Then Father plopped her across
the bed and called the family doctor. Mr.
Barnes guarded her until the doctor arrived
with his black bag, which held what my
mother suspected to be a dart gun. Her
screams rang throughout the house. Mr.
Barnes held her down while the doctor examined her.

"You all want me to be blue again!" she shrieked. "That's how you like it, right? Well, think again, you sons-abitches. You can't love me one week and bring this goddamn quack into my bedroom the next. Yes! I hit her! And I'll hit her again. That soul-stealing bitch. Frederick, come get me out of here. Get this son-ofabitch quack and his goddamn needle out of my bedroom. I watch *Wild Kingdom*, you bastard. I'll not take it. Come get this man, Frederick! He's trying to look in my blouse! Come get him!"

Father had gone to the study, and was on the phone with his lawyer. When I was old enough to understand legalities, Father would tell me that the woman had been escalating her charges against Mother. I sat on the study sofa with my hands under my thighs. I remember how cold my hands were. I began to fear that Mother was about to be taken from us, never to return. Every time now that my hands are cold and I warm them with my body, I remember my father's voice on the telephone, his trembling fingers on top of the desk. I figured he must be thinking the same thing as I was, that she would soon be strait-jacketed and hauled away. I knew about strait-jackets from watching movies on television with my brother that I had no business watching. Then I worried that her troubles might evolve into a seizure, like the one I had heard about that happened to a child in the school playground and someone had to run to the cafeteria to get a spoon to put in his mouth. I wondered if I should run to the kitchen and supply my mother with a spoon in case she tried to bite her tongue in two. I was full of anxiety, so full, in fact, that I was weighted down in my seat. I could not move. I remember Uncle Lawrence arriving, asking me where my mother and his father were. I pointed to the ceiling. He bounded upstairs. Father, had he been thinking, would have sent me to my room. Pearl was in her room, in tears, blaming herself because she had let Mother get out of the house. There was nobody available to comfort her. I planned to, once I heard everything Father said.

"Jesus, Daniel," he remarked to his lawyer on the other end of the phone. "She's sick. She's been sick. She got out of the house, and that woman was just in the wrong place at the wrong time."

My father listened for a moment and then he spoke again. "You know she wasn't trying to murder the damn woman. Is she still hysterical? How bad's her hip?"

The lawyer talked some more, and then my

father started crying into the phone. I had never seen him cry. I had seen him, lately, so frustrated over Mother's condition that tears would have been appropriate, but he had not shed a single one. He had let Mother do all the sobbing, and the screaming, and the loud agonizing. He suffered in silence, with an occasional "God damn" or "My life is not my own." I drew much of my solidity from him. If he had buckled under the weight of Mother's illness, perhaps I would have, too. And seeing him break down that day caused me to let go of everything I had been holding in. He was not a weak man or a man whose emotions were near enough the surface to trigger an outpouring. I knew Mother's dilemma was truly terrible when he cried.

He continued talking. "Not as sick as this. Not like this. It's never gotten this out of hand before."

More listening. He took his handkerchief out and blew his nose.

"You really think it'll come to that? Where would they want her to go?"

The lawyer must have said she would go to Dorothea Dix, the state hospital in Raleigh.

"God damn, Daniel," Father said. "She's not going there. I'll take her to Duke. See if that'll fix it, all right?"

That did fix it. She would go to Duke. Mother would not be taken to the asylum, which doubled as a drunk tank, according to some child I knew who spread the story that Luther Pipkin's father had dried out at Dix. I did not want my mother associating with the likes of the large, greasy, foulmouthed Mr. Pipkin.

Five

Twelve years earlier, after the postnatal obstetrical nursing staff told Father he would be charged a higher rate until Mother righted herself, he had made arrangements to put our farm in the care of an overseer for a few days so that he could stay with my mother around the clock. He knew he needed to be there in case she decided to really cut loose and do something. Although she could not have done anything at the hospital but infuriate the nurses, who were stuck taking care of her new baby, Father still worried about that possibility because she had listed so many times exactly what she would do if she were given free rein.

He said she would threaten to shoot, drown, smother, or gas herself, or at the very least, to run away from home.

Her obstetrician diagnosed her with the baby blues, a spot of postpartum depression, and told my father his presence would do her no good. He said she had been "momentarily struck," and that she would be fine once she was home and back in her own routine. I wonder about this particular obstetrician, how he could have examined my mother during the months prior to my birth without noticing that she was highly unusual. Perhaps he attributed her belief that I was going to be stillborn to coursing hormones. I am amazed that he had not phoned my father during the pregnancy to report a sideline diagnosis of mental illness. I imagine my mother flat on her back on an examining table, the doctor feeling her large belly. I hear her saying, "There's a dead baby in there. It's just gas causing my stomach to keep bumping up like that." What could he have been thinking? With that hint of incompetence in the doctor, I should consider myself lucky to have been born in one piece.

The doctor also told Father that it was not unheard of for a mother to reject her offspring initially. "There's no rule saying a woman has to adore that baby the minute she's born. The

whole experience is quite a shock for everyone, and then something of an anticlimax," he
said. Afterward the mother takes the baby
home, gets to know her a bit, and coos and
counts fingers and toes just like any other
mother. My mother, he predicted, would forget in a week's time that she had banished me.
The doctor also thought it best that I be bottle-
fed, as letting down milk had proven so difficult for her. Father wanted her to keep
trying, optimistic as he was in spite of everything. The doctor consented to allow Mother
to stay "wet" and then "dry up" on her own.
He instructed Father to cater to her wishes and
make sure she had plenty of help with me.
Fatigue could cause these baby blues to linger
and worsen.

Unless she was on a manic roll, Mother had
never done anything fatiguing, at least since
Pearl was hired. She supervised Pearl each
spring and summer day as they fed anywhere
from twenty to thirty field hands on picnic ta-
bles under the big pecan tree in our backyard.
Feeding and cleaning up after these men occupied the greater part of Pearl's day. She
oftentimes went about her business with me
on her hip. In fact, Pearl picked me up and
carried me around the house and yard every
day until my dangling feet reached her knees.

I remember that she was carrying me through the house when I reached up and pulled out my first tooth. She was compensating for the infrequency of my mother's touch.

Usually, Pearl had to stay up nights working if there was anything such as canning or darning to be done. In the winter, when the workforce was reduced to a few hired men who tended the livestock and mended fences, Mother was completely off duty. Pearl always took advantage of the time she saved—with fewer mouths to feed—to clean out the closets, wax the hardwood floors, lemon-oil the furniture, things like that. But Mother never went about looking to create jobs for herself. That is, she never went about looking unless she was manic. Father said that once when she was sick, when Freddy was four, and there was no Pearl there to monitor her, he came in from work to find that she had made Hubert remove and polish every brass doorknob in the house. The knobs came off more easily than they went back on, so many of the doors did not close properly after that day. She took a nice nap each afternoon, and if she was well, she would deal with the Nash County version of tinkers, with knife sharpeners and the candy man, who also sold wigs, and with Jehovah's Witnesses and the steady stream of al-

coholic day-laborers who showed up wanting
a dollar from my father. She would sit on the
back steps with the tenant farmers' children
and pick splinters out of their feet or teach
them to add by playing dominoes with them.
She would read whatever books were current
and then walk to Miss Woodward's house and
lend them to her. She built up quite a library,
when other families on Bend of the River
Road, such as my aunt and uncle's, had only
door-to-door-peddled encyclopedias, animal
husbandry manuals, and home remedy
guides. Had she not surmised that a roomful
of children day after day would grind on her
nerves, she would have made a wonderful
teacher. She had the requisite intelligence and
energy. Although I have no memory of her
reading to me, she did surround me with
books, and she never censored my choices. I
received my self-esteem in academics from
Freddy, my father, and Pearl.

If Mother was addled, she would interfere
with Pearl's chores. "She would put her hands
all in everything," Pearl told me, "and I would
have to take them out and fool her away from
the kitchen on some notion or other until I
could get a meal fixed and look after her."
Pearl would have to leave her kitchen duties
to baby-sit Mother, to follow her around the

house and the garden, like a spy, making sure she did not leave the premises. If Mother was depressed, she stayed in bed and let Pearl manage the feeding of the field hands and shoo the door traffic away. She would arise every now and then in the night, to bump around the house like a vaguely irritable ghost of uncertain origin.

When my father had spoken with the nursing staff and the obstetrician around the time I was born, he knew there was nothing temporary about Mother's affliction. He had been looking after her for too long. He did not see the need to broadcast the news that at times she went quite out of her mind. He would not have seen the worth in "going around telling everybody." There were some things people of my father's generation did not talk about, mental illness and cancer and assorted female troubles among them. Mother's distress was the business of the family, and my father limited talk about her violently rotating condition to people who had daily contact with her. Others did not need to know. He kept her loosely tethered on the farm, except for those extreme instances when he locked her in the house. He treated her as though she were a wayward cow, and when she strayed, when, for example, she made some long-distance phone calls and pestered strangers whose names she read in the society column of the Raleigh newspaper, he checked her. She was known to families on Bend of the River Road simply as "the Barnes woman with all the problems."

After an extra three days in the maternity ward with me, Mother was discharged in what Pearl believed to be dangerous shape. She told me that Mother came home all "jumbledy." The morning she was to leave the hospital, my father found her perched on the side of her bed, wearing brand-new clothes and a full face of makeup, ready to go home that instant. She announced that she was feeling as good as she looked and hoped that none of the nurses ruined her mood before she could check out. A department store clerk whom my mother traded with had sent over a purple felt hat with a black veil, a midnight-blue suit with black piping of a cowgirl sort on the collar and cuffs, and black satin pumps. The clerk was probably not even surprised when my mother requested that these items be delivered to her maternity bed. Mother was not able to button the new skirt, and so she got a rubber band from a nurse and rigged it as a closure. This created a large opening on her side that she declared nonexistent when my father brought it to her attention. He reconsidered the gap and agreed with her, hoping her jacket would drape low enough to spare her embarrassment when she walked down the hall.

She went to the mirror, applied even more makeup, and then turned and stood self-righteous, indignant, and generally irked, with her hands on the hips of her gaped-open skirt. A nurse, she told Father, had brought me into her room earlier that morning and tried to show her how to bathe me and care for my cord, clean my cradle cap, and keep milk from collecting behind my ears. This was a routine service for all mothers, even if, like my mother, they had someone hired to mind all the details.

"Do I look like an idiot?" she asked my father. "Don't I look like I know what to do with a baby? I took care of Freddy in a goddamn Quonset hut!"

She had given birth to my brother at an Army hospital in Louisiana when Father was overseas, finishing his last stint. I wonder how great a job she actually did with Freddy, without Pearl there to help her swab hydrogen peroxide on his umbilical cord. I wonder this because his belly button has always looked like the kind that little unkempt sharecropper children have. He habitually tugged at the waist of his bathing trunks, which he wore with the drawstring tied high on his stomach, preferring the risk of being called "high-pockets" to having his navel stick out.

I see my mother in that Quonset hut, in one of her wilder interludes, oblivious to Freddy and his tiny needs. She might have been too agitated to rest him on her lap and clean his head with cod liver oil and a soft brush. The way she bounced her knees, working her calves like springs, if she had put him on her lap she might have catapulted him right off into the air. In his baby pictures, dressed as he is in those white petit-point gowns, Freddy looks slightly dirty, and sad, as if he knows his cradle cap and cord and circumcision wound are not being properly tended to.

My father drove home from the hospital with me in his lap because he was afraid that my mother would squeeze me too hard or toss me out the window, whatever streaked through her mind. When we arrived at the house, only Mr. Barnes, Aunt Menefee, and Uncle Lawrence were waiting for us. Ordinarily, neighbors would have been invited to a home to see a new baby, but Father had sent word out that Mother had had some difficulties. He was probably hoping that people would think she had had a cesarean. Everybody would have to wait to view me. Uncle

Lawrence and Aunt Menefee knew the truth about how she had acted in the hospital, and not wanting to get tangled up with her, they had sent her a card, which Pearl kept with my baby memorabilia. It read, "See you soon."

My father turned me over to Pearl, who swept me upstairs, away from suffocating cigarette smoke. Then he attempted to monitor my mother so that she would not cut Aunt Menefee. He was not completely effective. Aunt Menefee complimented me, and then, as if in response, Mother spun around, ignoring her, to start a conversation with Uncle Lawrence. Mr. Barnes noticed my mother was ill, and he moved forward to help her, to distract her.

Everyone was quiet until Mr. Barnes spoke up.

"Aye God, Maggie, that's some suit you've got on."

Mother beamed and told everyone how much it cost. Aunt Menefee winced. Even when there was only family around, she could be embarrassed by Mother's candor.

"Then that's my coming-home present," Mr. Barnes said.

She did not thank him. She asked around if anybody had seen Freddy. Mr. Barnes told her that Freddy had run and hidden under the bathroom sink when Father drove up, and that he should be left there. "And don't let Pearl take him any supper under the goddamn sink," he said. After Mr. Barnes left, Freddy wet his pants, and Pearl had to drag him out of his hiding place by main strength.

Mother announced that she felt she was about to burst out of her clothing. "I'm fat," she declared.

Aunt Menefee reminded her that she had just had a baby. "It takes a while to get the weight off," she said.

Mother snapped, "What's your excuse?"

Aunt Menefee left the house and waited in the car for Uncle Lawrence. My father watched while Mr. Barnes held my mother's elbow, steered her upstairs, and took her into the nursery, this newly created space that she did not even notice. She did not remark on the Bambi mobile, and she did not appear to see the convertible bathtub-and-changing-table or any of Aunt Menefee's party presents. Whether she actually did take note of the new items and decided to withhold her gratitude or whether she was oblivious to outside circumstances simply because of the turmoil in her head, I am uncertain. I suspect the latter. I have no memory of her ever thanking Pearl outright for anything she did for her. Pearl never seemed to mind. Mr. Barnes took me from Pearl's arms and put me in my mother's. She sat in the window seat that looked out over the front yard.

"Maggie," Mr. Barnes said, "you need to ease your mind and feed your baby. She's going to look like her mother. Let's sit down and you feed that baby." They examined my hands and toes for a while, and then, when my mother was calmed, she unbuttoned her jacket and her satin blouse with no thought to his presence in the room. Mr. Barnes turned away and let me nurse until I was full. His effect on her was almost hypnotic. Pearl described it to me later: "She stopped being mad or fast or whatever you want to call what she was being that day. It took a very few minutes for her milk to let down." Mr. Barnes told Pearl not to bother me until my mother was through and to go downstairs and send my uncle to town for a case of lager. He learned, somehow, during his service in World War I, that German mothers drank it to bolster their milk supply. Uncle Lawrence drove to Rocky Mount and back, and my mother drank a lager with her lunch every day. For the next month she nursed me every few hours, and I became a very fat little baby.

Years later, when I found out I was pregnant with my first child, I phoned my brother in Charlotte and he congratulated me, and then teased that I would need to follow a parenting handbook, as I had learned so little methodology from my mother. He told me that if I did what Pearl did my baby would grow up fine. But there was a serious undercurrent to his teasing, that implication of our mother's lack of involvement with me when I was young, malleable, and forming my views of my family and the world. I asked him to elaborate.

"I remember," he said, "that when you first came home, we all had to be quiet so she could stay calm enough to nurse you. Pearl was on me constantly. And except when Mother was feeding you, she ignored you as much as she ignored me."

Because he was six years older than I was, I trusted his memory. Even though by that time I had forgiven Mother, I wanted to know more about my daily life with her. He said that generally, in the mornings, she would seem mildly happy about me, but by midday the novelty would have worn off. She did have enough responsibility to buy clothes for me, but he never stood by her in a department store and got the impression that she felt joy over buying pretty things for her baby. She

would let Pearl hold me while she rounded up
clothes, never smiling, just doing her business.

"I think she felt assigned to buy things for
you. You were a generic child of sorts," he told
me. "It was as though all the Barnes family,
with all those great-uncles and nieces and
nephews and cousins once and twice removed, collected from four corners of Nash
County, had drawn names at Christmas and
Mother had chosen a slip that said 'Hattie,
Baby Girl of Frederick's.' "

On many afternoons, Freddy would come
home from school to find Pearl taking care of
me, while my mother slept, read, shopped, or
visited with Mr. Barnes, who always took time
away from his enterprises to drive her to town
for a hot dog or hand-dipped ice cream at
Woolworth's. If it is indeed true that a person's character is decided in the first four
years of life, then Pearl was my salvation. As
she cooked, Freddy said, I played at her feet,
and she made pallets for me by the stove. They
both watched me growing up in the kitchen.
Pearl did her housework according to my
schedule, vacuuming the upstairs when I was
asleep in the kitchen, running the electric ap-
pliances when I was coloring or looking at
books at my little wooden table in the corner.
Father would come in and ask my mother

about my day, and she was apt to answer, "I have no idea. Ask Pearl." He finally learned to skip Mother entirely and go straight to Pearl.

I think about this now, about my mother's ignorance of my days. Now I understand her preoccupation with her own sanity. But when I grew old enough to realize that Mother was tossing my father's questions off to Pearl, I felt as if she were responding to the question of what sort of day my puppy had had. Pearl would always cheerfully report to Father whatever she and I had done together, and now, thinking back, I recall that she made it sound as though every puzzle I had put together alone had been put together under my mother's adoring gaze. Pearl would stretch the truth so that Miss Maggie would appear a more willing and active participant in motherhood than she actually was. I think Pearl did not want to hurt my father, to disappoint him. She wanted him to think the best of his wife whenever possible. She was good to all of us that way.

Freddy admitted that Pearl also controlled the considerable hostility he had toward me when I first came home. Had he been three and not almost seven, he would have thrown a fork at me. Instead, he slipped in a kick at the leg of my wicker bassinet each time he walked by it. Pearl took him aside and promised to jerk him if he did not stop. He told her with his own special irony, developed so young, that I was just what the household needed. Pearl was alarmed at his insight, but that did not mean she wanted to hear his views, so she pulled him into the pantry and gave him one of her talks. After that, his attitude toward me was fairly equable. Father had given her carte blanche in the discipline department. She could have twisted his ears off his head if she had wanted to.

Six

If my mother had not been married during those six weeks of 1967, if she had been just another untreated manic depressive, God knows how many men she could have wasted and what sort of trouble she could have found herself in at some place like Mr. Barnes's pool hall. Looking at the newspaper in the mornings, she commented on men, saying this one or that would be fine, with some minor grooming adjustments. During her manic spree, she had to be kept away from church, where a handsome new minister was causing jealous husbands all over Nash County to degrade their wives, to undermine their self-esteem to the point that they could not ever imagine such an attractive man finding them anything but dull-witted, saddle-bagged, and tiresome. My mother came back from the first service he preached, and at the noon meal, in front of the entire family, told my father the minister had not been able to keep his eyes off her.

Father said, "You're a pretty woman, Maggie."

"It was more than that, Frederick. It went deeper," she told him.

"You need to come upstairs. The children are here."

"Yes, take me upstairs," she said. "Come over here and carry me up the steps the way you're supposed to."

Father bent over and lifted Mother right out of her chair and took her to their bedroom. Pearl fixed them a light supper on a tray. They did not emerge until morning.

Sometime during this manic period, Freddy remade his room into a low-class version of a bachelor pad. I noticed that he would not help me with my schoolwork in there. By the time I was in school, his anger over my intrusion into the household had worn off enough for him to offer to check my work and give advice. But now he would help me only in my room, and if we needed any *World Book*s or *American Heritage*s of his, he brought them by the armload and dropped them on my bed. This was uncharacteristic of him, territorial as he was over books, always reminding me not to dog-ear pages.

He was eighteen by then, and knew some things about sex, but obviously not as much as he wanted to know, so he stole Hubert's off-brand pornographic magazines from the garage apartment and hid them in his room. When Pearl decided one day to clean out Freddy's monthly backlog of dirty clothes, she stepped inside the room to find that magazines had been torn apart, and pictures of trailer-park-looking girls were pasted, pinned, and taped everywhere. Pearl went berserk, crying, "Oh golly my God. Somebody help me!" I heard her and ran upstairs to see why she was so distressed. When I got to the landing, I stopped and considered whether I wanted to continue. The way she sounded, she might have just found my mother dead. I could not keep myself away, so I went on up the stairs and was relieved to see Pearl screaming outside Freddy's room, where Mother never went. With her big body, she kept Olive on the other side of the door, saying nobody decent was coming in. She shouted for my father, who raced to the doorway, where Mother was already, pushing Pearl aside to get through. I heard him ask if Freddy had a girl in there.

"No sir, Mr. Barnes," she said, "there's several."

Father moved her out of the way, and while he muttered "God damn" over and over, Pearl dogged his heels, warning him to get control of Mother or the house would fall apart. Freddy was already feeling her influence, she told him.

"This whole family will go straight to ruination," she continued.

When they went downstairs to discuss exactly how to rein in Mother, I peeked at Freddy's walls. I had no real idea what I was looking at. All the girls looked sad, made up like clowns. They looked like they needed a nice bath and a good supper. They seemed foreign to me. I did not make the connection between the essence of those photographs and what I had heard from my parents' bedroom. Looking back, I realize there is little doubt that our house was suffused with sex. Olive was all but locked in her room at night by Pearl, who suspected, I suppose, that she would follow Mother's lead after having heard day in and day out how good it felt. Father made

Freddy remove the pictures himself and repair the damage done to the walls. For days he was not allowed to close his door, not even when he was changing clothes.

There was, I sensed, something going on in the house that I was not privy to. Conversations and events seemed to swirl above my head. My mission was to eavesdrop on the life of the house, but whenever I came close to having my concerns answered, Father and Pearl would turn their backs to me and speak in quieter tones. Pearl detected my curiosity and confusion and took it upon herself to explain sex to me. She spoke to me hurriedly one morning, just before school.

"Hattie," she said, "people practice having babies. Lots of people spend a lot of their time practicing. Your mother, lately she's been liking to practice. One of these days she'll catch her breath."

That told me nothing. All I thought was that my mother was in a running sweat to have another baby. She was practicing all day every day. She was starting to look worn around the edges, and I thought of the story I had overheard Uncle Lawrence telling my father about the octogenarian Senator Walsh, whose body had been removed from a Pullman car in Rocky Mount six hours after he had married his young secretary and boarded the Orange Blossom Special at Washington's Union Station for his Florida honeymoon. Father and Uncle Lawrence laughed uproariously. That girl had killed that old man, and now my mother was killing my father, slowly, causing him to run and hide from her in the sanctity of Miss Woodward's home. My mother was really quite powerful, I thought, to be able to kill with her body this way.

Her sleeping schedule became erratic, and she started smoking and drinking more than usual. She seemed to enjoy both immensely. Mr. Barnes brought her cartons of Salems, telling my mother that smoking mentholated cigarettes would settle her nerves better than drinking would. Still, she turned to liquor late at night when everybody was asleep. My father stayed downstairs with her, sleeping on the sofa; he swore that he would be able to hear her should she attempt to unbolt a door to get outside. Pearl sat up as late as she could at the kitchen table with her, emptying ashtrays, listening to my mother's version of why the two races were having such problems, beating each other over the head from Birmingham to Chicago. Pearl remembered years later that Mother's explanation had something to do with people's inability to open their

souls to truth and beauty, but that was all she
could understand. One night when Mother
had hit the bourbon a little too hard, she
begged Pearl to explain why colored and
white people could not get along, and in this
moment of expansive camaraderie, Pearl said,
Mother let her stroke her hair and talk to her
like a baby. Then, in a frightening flash, she
turned on Pearl, telling her she had never
liked the way she washed the shower doors,
and if she did not want to find her ass on the
street the next day, she could get upstairs, yes,
right now at three o'clock in the morning, and
chamois-cloth every goddamn shower door in
the house. Pearl said that was when she
poured three fingers of bourbon for herself.

It was rare enough for Mother to be at
breakfast, but one morning during these six
weeks of mania she was at the table drunk. I
think that in this instance she was using alcohol as a means of bringing her elevated
mood down a notch or two. She never drank
when she was low, probably intuiting the in-
herent depressive effect of alcohol. She jabbed
out a cigarette on her plate and asked me if I
was ten or eleven. I told her I was twelve.
Then she wanted to be reminded when my
birthday was so she could buy a present. I told
her, and then she demanded to know what I

wanted. I said I had not made up my mind. She asked me again, with greater impatience. She was pushing me hard, and I knew that whatever I said to her was going to be wrong. It was as though I had been walking down a street and had had my sleeve yanked by a vagrant who wanted something I did not have in my pockets to give, some money, some cigarettes, or some food. My mother's insistence that I decide on a birthday present kept pace with my mounting frustration, and when I had heard more than I could bear, I forgot my father's stoicism and cried. Pearl walked in and asked what was happening.

"My daughter here doesn't give a damn about her birthday," Mother told Pearl as she sat there weaving in her chair.

"I'm sure she does," Pearl countered. "It's just that it's early yet."

"Yeah, but she still doesn't give a damn. You can't do a thing for somebody like that. Freddy's that same goddamn way. Slipping around me all the time. Hiding things."

"She's not hiding her birthday. Are you, Hattie? She just wants you to feel better and not load you up with things to do. I'll take you to town shopping when the time comes." Pearl, I could tell, wanted the conversation to end before Mother started to cry along with me.

But Mother cried anyway. Her hands shook as she lit another cigarette. "All I want to do is buy her a present."

"You can do that. Don't worry now." Pearl rubbed Mother's back.

I grabbed my books and ran out the door and sat on the front steps, waiting for the school bus, trying to pull myself together before it arrived. I remember wishing that she would pass out and stay out until I went to bed that evening. I did not want to see her face for a while. Even out on the steps, I could hear Mother telling Pearl that she had a child with no goals, a child who ought to have every goddamn page in the F. A. O. Schwarz catalogue turned down, but no. I had to move all the way out to the road before I could no longer hear the sound of my mother screaming about the freakishness of a child who had no idea what she wanted for her birthday. But I knew what I wanted: my own subscription to *National Geographic* and a new Madame Alexander doll for the collection my father was accumulating for me. And although I would not have acknowledged it at the time, I wanted her as well. I wanted her because of that irrational component of love that made

me want to be near her, even as she maintained a steady and predictable distance from
me.

At times like these, Pearl poured nearly
toxic levels of alcohol into Mother, trying
somehow to make whatever damage she was
doing to the family stop before it ground us
all down. Pearl told me once how she would
check Mother's pulse as she lay on the bathroom floor and cover her with an afghan, and
then wait, rest and wait. In less time than it
took a Bowery bum to shake off Saturday
night, my mother would come out and start
raising hell again. Olive threatened Pearl with
moving back to Jonesboro every time Mother
accused her, totally without justification, of
laying up with Hubert, keeping him from
pruning the oleander bushes and raking
leaves, but Pearl would remind Olive of what
Jonesboro held for her if she were to return:
brothers, uncles, cousins, and groping suitors,
all as shiftless as Hubert. She asked Olive how,
if she could not bear my mother, did she ever
hope to bear a gap-toothed man of the sort
who would materialize from the swamps and
come pester her the minute she got to town?
During those six weeks of mania, my mother
thought she heard Olive "backmouthing" her,
and hit her on the side of the face with a fly-

swatter. Mother had asked Olive about some brown streaks on white clothing, and she had blamed the washing machine, which as it turned out did have a rust problem. But Mother was sure that Olive had been deliberately ruining clothes. After accusing Olive of stealing her silver compact, Mother pinched the top of her hand and drew a blood blister the size of a dime. But Olive endured it all.

When Mother was not in bed with my father, or drunk, she was going into one department store and coming out of another on a spending spree. Just as he did when Mother was "normal," Mr. Barnes chauffeured her and followed her around, paying for whatever she heaped on counters. In that one period, Pearl saw ten dresses, five suits, ten pairs of shoes, five handbags, several silk nightgowns and matching robes, and every satin brassiere in Mother's size come home. She had Mr. Barnes take her to the book department at Belk's, where she told the clerk to bag every hardcover novel published in the last three months, and to give the bill to the gentleman with her. She also bought several new pieces of furniture, including a sleigh bed and a dresser for her room. We talked about her manic splurges when I was an adult, and she was not able to recall whether Mr. Barnes tried to stop her, or even slow her down. He loved pleasing her, and this urge must have overridden any need he might have seen either to try to adjust her mood himself or to seek professional help for her. And as Father has so often told me, sometimes when Mother was ascending into full mania she could be a joy to be around. She could be chatty and vivacious. Mr. Barnes no doubt had a fine time squiring her about town, dressed as she would have been in a stylish suit, high heels, and seamed stockings. She wore seamed black stockings until the stores stopped carrying them. Mr. Barnes pleased her most by taking her to Hertzberg Furs and to A Stone's Throw jewelry store. Townspeople who did not know them might have thought he was her sugar daddy. They might have wondered if she would board a train with him and cause his corpse to be hauled off somewhere down the line. Father bought her a few baubles to try to keep pace with Mr. Barnes, but he could have saved his money.

When I once noticed that there were no pictures in the family albums of my sixth birthday, which fell during a manic cycle, I asked Mother why. She said that she did not remember it. She changed the subject, moving quickly on to anything that did not remind her of how sick she actually could be. She seemed ashamed, as if the missing pictures symbolized an abandonment. It was not that something had happened to the camera and another one was not bought in its place. In 1949, at a going-out-of-business sale, Mother bought eight or nine Brownies at once. This might have been the only multiple purchase she made that was not the result of a compulsion. She bought them as insurance against her tendency to misplace things. She would put her belongings in wildly illogical places, and my father could not help her search for whatever she was missing at the moment, because without logic there were no clues.

"Okay, Maggie," he would have said. "Where were you the last time you had the camera?"

"I have no idea. Things drop from my brain."

"Then I cannot help you," he would have responded.

He got very frustrated with her when she could not find things, as though he momentarily forgot that she had so many other items swirling around unorganized up in that brain. He would shout, "Now, Maggie!" whenever she lost his Swiss Army knife. She borrowed it to cut threads on her needlepoint and lost it repeatedly. He stopped lending her things like nail clippers and handkerchiefs, and she said herself that this was probably a good rule. She generally retained such self-awareness about her illness, her shortcomings, and her absent-mindedness. She had to be very ill to lose the awareness, and when she did not know she was sick, she was in terrible form. But Mother never became anxious about things she lost. The solution was always simple. Her world was so complicated by the illness that she must have been grateful to have at least one problem that could be solved with money.

She was never one for searching for something when a replacement could be gotten. She would have said, "Yes, you can help me, Frederick. Go to the guest room closet and get another Brownie." Father would have done as she asked.

Only Pearl could divine that my mother must have put her pink slippers in the liquor cabinet or a book under the sink or a magazine on top of the refrigerator.

"I never tried to figure out where she put anything, like in saying, 'Well, she was reading a cookbook so she probably put it under the sink,' " Pearl told me. "Ha! All I did was think of the one place it would never occur to

me to put a magazine, or a pair of sunglasses,
or whatever she was missing. Needlepoint? In
the basement! Black stockings? Under the bed!
I always found what she lost."

Father has told me that Mother actually took
two rolls of film at my sixth-birthday party,
which was attended only by Mr. Barnes and
Aunt Menefee's family. And then she acted on
the belief that she was capable of all things,
even developing film.

She went into the bathroom and shook the
film out of the camera and dropped both canisters into a sink full of something she knew
would work, like rubbing alcohol. I see her sitting in her slipper chair, chain-smoking, looking at herself in the mirror every time she gets
up to check on the film.

She soon forgets why the canisters are soak-
ing, so she drains the sink and throws them
away. She feels like washing her face but cannot decide if she would rather do that or buy
a piano so she can play anything she wants to,
which she believes she can do, given the
chance, which she had as a girl although she
never performed with distinction at the recit-
als. But that would not be the case now, not
with the music of the spheres in her head. All
she has to do is listen, and her fingers will go
up and down the keyboard automatically. Just

like typewriting. She wants to play something fast and complicated. A rhapsody. She can already feel the music starting to flow through her left arm. It is tingling with inspiration. Or is something crawling up her sleeve? What would she wear when she played? That is very important, to look professional. Her left arm, the one with something, bugs or inspiration or whatever the hell it is, shoots over her head, as though she is the first student in the class to think of the answer. Her arm comes back down. She sits on her hand, so it will not try to go anywhere. Her arm feels as if it could rotate, or is it revolve, completely off her shoulder, and she does not like that.

All she wants to do is get dressed up. She has the perfect recital gown. In fact, she has two closets packed with dresses Mr. Barnes has bought for her, many still with the tags on them because Frederick rarely takes her anyplace where he would allow her to wear sequins. She sees herself in one dress after another, and she is beginning to wish things would slow down a bit. She wants to crawl up on the sink and stare at the pores on her face.

A thought moves so quickly from one side of her brain to the other that she cannot catch it long enough to lure it out to its end. Trying to make a thought stop, just one, makes her

feel faint. Whew! That was hard work! I see
her collapsing on the slipper chair, almost
breaking it, and lighting a cigarette. Frederick
lets her smoke when she goes fast. Bless him.
Bless the gift of music in her soul. She thinks
how what she really wants to be is a poet. She
would have to go to New York, and that
would mean packing. She could just get drunk
instead, but then she would vomit. It would
be very hard to write poems down on a piece
of paper when words fly away like scared rob-
ins from their nest. It would not be as easy as
playing concert classics on the piano. Should
she fly to New York? That would be grand.
Then she would land. Grand and land. See?
She does some mental packing, trying to figure out the season without going to the window to see the color and number of leaves on
the trees, and then my father comes in.

He said that he saw the ruined film in the
trashcan and got three Sominex from their hiding place. "I was doing us a favor," he told
me. "Otherwise, she would have terrorized us
all."

She grinned and cooed that she felt perfect,
actually better than perfect, and she saw life
so clearly now. She saw how everything in the
universe was made for a purpose and that
purpose would be revealed to her through

dreams. Then her job would be to tell people how to live to best please the Creator. She spoke for Him now.

Father told her the pills would make her feel even better, dream even deeper, and she took them happily. He waited there, listening for her to pause long enough on the poetry-of-the-universe jag to be coaxed to the bed, where he put her underneath the covers, still wearing her dress and stockings, so she could rest for her trip to New York. He humored her, as he thought worked best, next to Sominex, in these instances. Then he told her the birthday party was over and I was happy with my presents, particularly a Madame Alexander doll called Chatterbox. Then the Sominex kicked in. Mother's last words to him were, "See if the cedar shoe trees are in my blue pumps."

Father got up and hid the razor blades and haircutting scissors in Pearl's room. Then he put the Sominex, aspirin, and sundry other medications in his pants pockets. When she sped this way, sometimes she would say she was blessed with immortality, among other things. He rested beside her, still dressed himself. He did not go to sleep until Olive came in to take the second shift in the rocking chair in the corner. He said he felt as though he were trying to fall asleep on a troop ship. He could sense the disturbing commotion of my mother's dreams, and out of loyalty, he joined her in a miserable night. She woke up before daylight and had to be told where she was. Whenever she awakened very sick, she thought she was in a hotel room. Nothing, none of the intimacies of their life together, wedding pictures, the silver-framed invitation, seemed familiar to her. Father always hoped they would soon.

Seven

The day of the crash, while Mother screamed at the doctor, Father ended the conversation with his lawyer, then came over to me, sat down, and cried on my shoulder, as if I were his mother, or at least a person his size. I patted him on the back, and then I said I wanted to go upstairs with Pearl and Freddy. My blouse was wet with his tears.

I locked myself in Freddy's room and told him everything Father had said on the phone. Freddy had been lying facedown on his bed. He sat up and pretended to be as stoic as Father usually was. Then he began sorting out the conversation for me. He pitched his analysis at my level, simplifying the language, though not the concepts.

"The woman Mother hit wants to bring all these charges against her," he said, "but the lawyer's thinking that if the doctor can have her declared insane or something, he can get everything dropped. And maybe then the newspaper won't follow the story. If she wasn't a Barnes, they'd leave her alone."

I knew that Mother was insane. Even at twelve, I could see how a driving adventure that might have been called an antic could take a nasty turn. I had seen words pour out of her in a furious torrent, and I had heard her proclaim too many great schemes for organizing everything from the United Nations to her coat closet. I had seen her set up the ironing board in her bedroom and press Father's shirts two and three times even though Pearl had already ironed them perfectly. Mother had, in the past, taken as many as five or six showers a day, and she would wash her hands at the kitchen sink countless times with the water pouring over her arms, like a surgeon prepping. Freddy and I knew that she was not like other people, but we did not want strangers in town or teachers and students at our school to get a glimpse at the disarray inside our house. Freddy told me what her evaluation would involve. I believed that he knew these things from reading detective magazines and watching late-night movies on television.

"Some doctor will give her a bunch of tests and see what's wrong with her. Then he'll tell the judge, 'Yes, this woman was off her rocker when she knocked over that woman with the car.' Then the whole thing will be dropped."

"But what about Mother?" I asked.

"They'll straighten her out."

"How?" And who is "they," I wondered.

"I can't say," Freddy told me.

I thought he knew. He knew, and it was too awful to tell me. Each year, his class took a field trip to Raleigh to see, among other official things, the electric chair in the medieval fortress known as the State Correctional Institution. Somehow, I got the impression that criminals were not always electrocuted all the way, or to effect, that they were sometimes only tortured. Also, I thought the chair was a sort of wired dunce affair. Lurid tales trickled down through the school and, for a time, acted as a deterrent against children's stealing pencils and erasers from the school store, where I worked each day before homeroom.

I ran out of Freddy's room and into Pearl's. Both she and Olive were in the room, which was sparsely decorated with an oval braided rug on the hardwood floor and a vase of plastic flowers and school pictures of Jonesboro nieces and nephews on the dresser. Pearl was sitting on the edge of her bed, and Olive was in a ladder-back chair near the window. Both of them were sobbing into handkerchiefs as big as baby diapers. I went over and sat by Pearl. She crammed her handkerchief down the front of her dress, leaving most of it hanging out, like a bib, and put her arm around me.

"I let your mother escape," she said, "and look what happened."

I told her it was not her fault.

Olive sniffled. "I've been telling her that. I was right here and didn't see or hear a thing, and then she was gone." Olive went on to say that if Pearl was at fault, so was she. They wanted, I thought, for me, as a representative of the Barnes family, to release them from responsibility. At least Olive did. Pearl, I believed, might blame herself indefinitely.

I told Pearl what Father had said on the phone and what Freddy had told me. I asked if what Freddy had said was true.

"I don't know," she responded. "All I want is for somebody to help her. She's in the sticks the worst I've ever seen her."

This was how Pearl described a situation in

which a person is overwhelmed by circumstance. When, for example, she had too many pots that needed to come off the stove at once, she would shout to Olive, "I'm in the sticks! Come help me!"

Pearl had always told me that Mother would get better one of these days, and I hoped that day had come. I wanted Maggie Barnes, the woman with all the problems, to turn into my mother, and although I was tired of waiting, I still hung on to Pearl's optimism about her improvement. If it took hitting a woman with the car to get Mother some help, then that was that. I do not remember feeling sorry for the woman, wondering about her condition, wondering whether she was in agony in the emergency room. I just wanted her to leave Mother alone so our family could concentrate on the impending hospitalization and recovery, as scary as it all sounded.

Pearl asked if I thought my father was going to be mad at her and Olive. "We can pack our bags and go today if he wants us to," she said.

I felt too small to be asked such a big question. Although I could not read Father's mind, I believed he was a fair man, and I knew that he knew just how sneaky Mother could be, how difficult she was to guard when she set her mind to do something. All three of us could still hear her yelling. Pearl hugged me to her chest, holding my head so tightly that it slid right down into her large cleavage, like a hand into bread dough. She reassured me that my mother would be taken care of, that I need not worry anymore. Mother would be given some medicine, and it was about time. Yes, it was surely time.

At least Mother was going to Duke, not to the Dorothea Dix State Hospital for the Insane, an emphatically Victorian-looking institution that sat on a hill on the bad side of Raleigh. Its proximity to the state correctional facility confirmed in my mind the unshakable belief that Dix patients and the criminally insane were shuttled back and forth from one facility to the other and perhaps lost in mazes of corridors. While I had never known anybody, except Mr. Pipkin, who had been "sent to Dix," I had heard Pearl read aloud from the morning paper about how drunken vagrants who were arrested for something like loitering with intent, and who were unable to produce identification or next of kin, were carted off to Dix to "undergo treatment." I got the impression that once checked in, a person did not leave, and I imagined that the inmates were fed slop on metal trays and had to eat with their hands, like those African children squatting on their haunches on CARE commercials, because they might stab themselves or one another with the sharpened end of a spoon.

The words "imbecile," "moron," "mongoloid," "idiot," and "retard" had not yet been sanitized in that big high-powered washing machine of the seventies, and one of my worst fears was that if my mother was sent to Dix she would be given an epithet she would never live down. Instead of being "the Barnes woman with all the problems," she might return, if they ever let her come home, branded a lunatic. In addition, she might have gone into Dix with her inoffensive compulsions, like ironing shirts and washing her hands, and then learned "in the stir" how to drool and mess herself. Just as a petty criminal goes into prison for stealing hubcaps and then is taught how to fashion murderous instruments out of breakfast utensils, my mother might have absorbed the attributes of the irredeemably deranged and become a monster.

I could hear my father's soothing voice in her room, and I was encouraged by the fact that he was with her, packing a bag for her, finding her satin slippers and several of the robes and nightgowns of recent purchase, readying her to go to Duke, where white people went for cancer, gallbladder, and cataract surgery. Colored people went to Chapel Hill, the teaching hospital. But for people like us, Duke was the only option. It was very expensive. I had no idea of the exact figure, but I did know it required a phone call to the bank to transfer funds from Mr. Barnes's checking account into my father's. I heard this call and was pleased that my mother had access to Mr. Barnes's deep pockets.

I felt certain that she would not pick up any unsavory traits from the other patients at Duke. The mayor's wife had had some sort of knee surgery there and was photographed at home amid her many spaniels, praising the doctors at Duke for saving her leg. Through the benevolence of the Jaycee and Kiwanis clubs, children were being flown in from behind the Iron Curtain—a screen I had just lately started to understand as a symbol rather than a width of chain mail hanging around Russia like a sheet of plastic suspended on a rod around a claw-footed bathtub—to have eyes uncrossed, and noses, lips, and palates created. Mr. Barnes had gone around the county from one store to another, replacing nickel-a-chance punchboards with fruit jars bearing scrawled demands to contribute money to send Ida Wheeler's boy to Duke. Ida Wheeler was a widow, whose husband had died when one of my grandfather's tractors turned over on him in a ditch. No picture of the palsied child was needed to inspire gamblers to put into Mr. Barnes's fruit jars what they would have bet on the punchboard. People could ride by the Wheeler house anytime and see the boy bound into his nineteenth-century wheelchair with calico strips, parked by Ida's side at the clothesline, or at the end of a garden row, or on the porch. I had seen him, too. With that blanket on his lap, he reminded me of the boy in *The Secret Garden,* and I fantasized that he spoke with an English accent, but he was just a dirt poor child twisted with scoliosis and in bad need of a brace. Mr. Barnes thought Duke could help him, because, like everybody else, he knew the doctors at Duke enjoyed a reputation as great as that of the swells at Johns Hopkins, where Virginians went because they were too snobbish to go anywhere but northward for treatment. He primed each jar with a five-dollar bill, and everybody knew that when Mr. Barnes collected the jars he would ask storekeepers for a full report of who had put in how much. Those who had not emptied their pockets would probably be turned away the next time they showed up at the back door of the pool hall, parched and trembling.

Mother was spared the humiliation of commitment because she went to Duke without resistance. She was too doped up to argue. Mr. Barnes and my father brought her out of the bedroom, or rather they dragged her along. They stopped at my door to tell me to come give Mother a kiss. I had heard schoolyard tales about children made to lean over coffins and kiss Grandma good-bye, which was precisely the feeling I had when I put my lips to my mother's cheek. Her skin did not feel like living, human flesh. It felt like frog skin, or old-nursing-home-patient skin. I squeezed her hand, not too hard, because I was afraid of putting my fingers completely through her flesh. Perhaps, I thought, all the liquor and cigarettes had sucked the splendid freshness and vigor out of Mother's skin. I knew enough about the properties of certain chemicals to realize that liquor was not unlike embalming fluid, something I had heard about from the daughter of the owner of the unfortunately named Bright's Funeral Home.

She had told me once, without my asking, that the skin of dead people did not snap back and her father had to "pump them full of stuff" to make them rosy and pleasing to the touch. She told me another time, again without solicitation, that her father occasionally worked on people with his head enclosed in a plastic bag, not for sanitary purposes, but to speed the dyeing process of his Grecian Formula 66. I thought that she had meant his whole head, not just his hair, and the vision of him going about his gruesome task with a bag over his head in the shuttered upstairs rooms of Bright's kept me up at night. This girl said she had touched many dead people, young and old, and that all skin, without exception, felt as though it could be moved from wrist to elbow and back again until her father took to work.

Youthful, smooth skin had always been a hallmark of Mother's vanity, and now I felt I could rub hers from her elbow all the way down to her new Rolex. She was like a dead woman about to be entombed wearing a thousand-dollar watch. She had always been careful about her appearance, buying the new miracle breakthrough products Helena Rubinstein offered each season. My mother did not merely clean her face, she *cleansed* it with a remoisturizing, vitamin-enriched, protein-enhanced overnight-wonder formula that cost five dollars for a bottle that lasted only about a month. That is, she did this to her skin when she was well. During her manic binge, nicotine and alcohol had ravaged her muscle tone and

popped vessels underneath her eyes. Had she
been able to focus on the mirror when Father
took her to the downstairs bathroom right before the long ride to Duke, she would have
cried over what the illness had done to her.
She had always been determined to beat age,
to avoid looking like the crones who sat
around us in church and offended her eyes
with their liver spots, hairy warts, sagging
chins, and mustaches.

But there Mother went, down the hall, aged
ten years in the six weeks that her mind had
just suffered her body to endure. I wondered
if Duke could take those years back. Could
they give her injections of the kind Pearl's
movie magazines said were given to hung-
over stars? Could they restore her the way Mr.
Bright pumped people up so that loved ones
could say the departed had never looked that
beautiful? I remember wanting Mother trans-
formed. I remember wishing her well, safe
journey, *bon voyage.*

Eight

As I have said, Mother was not always sick. She feared that teachers and PTA mothers suspected she was abnormal, so the instant she felt well, she would march off to Freddy's school and display her excellent mental hygiene. She never told me how these women treated her on her excursions into normality. I can only hope that they were kind to her and did not whisper before she had time to get out of a room. Pearl was the judge of whether Mother should go to the school. She would appraise her mental health and then make a decision, and as a rule, she was successful. But once, when Freddy was twelve, Mother fooled her.

"She seemed right," Pearl would later tell me. Mother informed Pearl that she had a lunchtime conference scheduled with Freddy's teacher. "She was dressed perfectly normal, too. That's what hoodooed me," Pearl said.

Freddy was at PE, playing softball, when Mother arrived. She appeared behind the batter's cage and waved at him as he sat on a bench, awaiting his turn.

"She looked ready for something. I didn't know what. It was one of those times when I knew she was on the verge of opening her mouth to say God knows what," Freddy told me. He tried to pretend she was not there, to wish her away, but every time he looked at home plate, there she was, a few feet in back, behind the cage, waving at him more and more insistently. He saw the coach walk up to her, perhaps to ask if he could help, and then he saw Mother shake her head and point to him. The coach went back to instructing the boys. Freddy stood and approached the plate, and as he took the bat from the catcher, he heard Mother hissing to get his attention.

"I waved at her," Freddy recounted. "I hoped that would satisfy her, hoped she would see me hit, and then leave."

He got into position and heard the coach telling him to back up, not to crowd the plate. He backed up. Then he heard Mother.

"He's not crowding the plate!" she shouted. "He can hit the ball any way he pleases!"

"Half the children were too horrified to open their mouths, and the others couldn't stop laughing," Freddy remembered. He said that he was so mad he could not cry.

The coach walked up to the wire fence and spoke to Mother again. This time, he pointed in the direction of the parking lot, where Hubert sat in the Oldsmobile waiting for her. Freddy said that at least she spared him the indignity of having all the children hear what she said when the coach motioned for her to leave. Only Freddy and the catcher heard her tell the coach, "You can go straight to hell." When she did leave, Freddy was excused from the game and made, so very unjustly, to sit on the bench. It took weeks for him to live down the episode, and the tale spread through the school like a runaway case of measles.

When he got home, Freddy took the risk of chastising Pearl for letting Mother get out of the house. Pearl was shocked, since Mother had both left and returned home beaming, as though she had expected and had received a glowing report from Freddy's teacher. Pearl stood in Freddy's room and let him work out his fury on her, and when she thought he should be through, she told him so. "I have heard enough," she said. Freddy turned to his homework and tried to put the day out of his mind so he could concentrate on his lessons. Pearl did bring him supper on a tray so he would not have to meet Mother at the table, and she told my parents that he was doing a project that was due the following day. Mother, Pearl said, never mentioned what had happened. When Pearl asked her how the school visit had gone, she responded, "Fine. Just fine."

From then on, Pearl was more alert to Mother's frame of mind anytime she announced a desire to visit the school.

"She had to have looked well in the face for a week, and then I had to see in her eyes if she was lying to me about meetings and such," Pearl told me.

If Pearl thought Mother should stay at home, she would dream up a variety of reasons to keep her there. Hubert was missing, or he had misplaced the car keys, or the car would not start. If Mother thought of asking Mr. Barnes to drive her, then Pearl had to bring out the big cannon. She would tell Mother outright that she thought she was on the sick side that day.

"She'd start heading for that phone to call Mr. Barnes, and I'd have to catch her and tell her she was not herself. I'd say, 'You might feel like yourself. But you are not yourself.' "

Usually Mother would take Pearl's advice and say there was always another day, but on one occasion she said, "You're right, Pearl. But I just want to go to that school and make up to Freddy for the way I am."

"And what way is that?" Pearl asked.

"Why, I'm crazy," she answered. "No child needs a crazy mother." When Pearl told me this, I pitied the truth that lay behind Mother's self-realization.

The autumn when I was six years old, Pearl judged Mother sane enough to respond to a call for volunteers. The woman who phoned our home told Pearl that she had sent all the children from school with a form. But as far as Pearl and Mother knew, Freddy had brought no form home. When I asked him what he had done with it, he told me that he'd thrown it away before he was out of the classroom. Volunteers were needed to decorate seasonal bulletin boards for the main hall, and the woman who phoned had been in high school with Mother and remembered her artistic ability: Mother had once won a creative arts award. Word of Mother's current temperament must not have reached her. Mother said she would gladly design and install the artwork, and Pearl was satisfied that Mother's streak of wellness would continue for a while.

Freddy was not so sure. He did not want the transformation from his sweet mother to the mother who could send a coach to hell to take place in front of his schoolmates. Although she did not put up anything outlandish or garish, I can hardly bear to imagine the stress she caused Freddy when she appeared at his school with her scissors and stapler and construction-paper cutouts of pumpkins and witches and Pilgrims and the like. She also worked a fill-in stint in the middle school library, which he saw not as an occasion for her to try to be something of a normal mother who would sit quietly and rubber-cement fresh card-holders into the backs of books but as another opportunity for her to mortify him. He was on the cusp of puberty at the time, and probably would not have wanted even an ordinary mother to show up at school. He told me years later that he was afraid of being summoned to the principal's office to find her slumped over in a chair, sobbing, in custody, caught roaming the halls. Other boys his age had dreams of being locked in cloakrooms

with pretty teachers, but Freddy had night-
mares about gigantic school officials scowling
down at him, asking him what he intended to
do about his mother, restless dreams of
Mother hovering behind the batting cage.

The spring after she created all those bulletin boards, she received a call saying that she
was to be given a volunteer's certificate at an
awards ceremony. She did not attend, because
she could not pull herself out of bed, but by
the time the certificate reached her in the mail,
she had cycled into a manic state. For some
undisclosed reason, the citation now infuri-
ated her. She tore it up and set fire to it, in
front of Freddy, in the kitchen sink. He would
never forget the flame's first touching the edge
of the paper. Then, a week later, she was better. She called the school and requested a replacement, explaining that the original citation
must have gotten lost at the post office. The
school sent another, and she had it framed and
hung it in the den alongside my father's Junior
Order and Progressive Farmer citations. She
hoped that people would read it and know
that at some time in some place she had been
happy and had gotten along well with others.

If it had not been for Pearl and Olive, my
father also might have become mentally ill.

He never did anything for himself. He had no hobbies, watched only a few television shows, and then only when Mother did not need him by her side. He enjoyed the evening news, and this period was set aside as his time, the hour of the day that belonged to him. But even then, my mother might interrupt and yell for him to come upstairs to get in bed with her or just sit by her. I used to wonder what went through his mind as he walked up those steps, wordlessly. Mother never called for Freddy or me, only for him, or if he was not at home, for Pearl. Sometimes I would hear her on the phone, telling Mr. Barnes, "You've got to come get me." He typically showed up right away to rescue her from whatever she believed she could not bear within the household or within herself. One of the first times I was not in a crib and could get out of my bed myself, I went to her when I heard her shout Father's name. He came to the door and excused me. Then they shut me out so that I could not see better what I had glimpsed through the crack in the door, my mother squatted in the corner with her feet under her, sobbing onto her knees. I remember standing there looking at my small face, made convex by the brass doorknob, and then running back downstairs to the kitchen, to

Pearl, who gave me a big piece of pineapple cake.

My father was the tiredest person I ever knew. He would frequently say that he woke up at three and did not sleep the rest of the night, listening for Mother's movements. She could be so sly. He lived on guard duty. When my mother seemed suspended in continuous pessimism, he would criticize himself, Pearl said, over his inability to improve her by loving her. His frustration was grinding and relentless, the cause of chronic dyspepsia, lower backaches, and other recurrent ailments. On top of the despair was his feeling that he had to be a bottomless pit of patience and tolerance traversing the course of Mother's volatile moods.

I was five when he brought home Fanny, a Jack Russell terrier, because Mother had said she wanted a puppy. Father was met with open, blinding hostility.

"That's not the kind of dog I wanted," she shouted.

"I thought you'd like it," he responded evenly.

I was standing in the kitchen with the two of them. Father handed me the puppy and told me to take it outside. I stood on the porch and listened.

"I'll take it back and see what else the breeder has," Father offered.

"Forget it," she said.

I started thinking that if I were Father, I would take the little dog back and make her do without a pet entirely. As cute as the animal was, that is what I thought he should do. But he kept talking to her, asking what sort of dog she would like instead. I had the feeling that he would go anywhere and pay any price for a suitable dog.

"I said just forget it," she told him.

Still in that even voice, Father said, "Okay, if that's how you feel about it, I'll take the dog back this afternoon."

"I don't care!" she shouted. "Just fuck you. Fuck you and your little dog, too."

I had no idea what she meant, but I stored the word away for later understanding. Father did not take the dog back right then. I stayed outside and played with it. By lunchtime, Mother was in tears, apologizing for being so nasty when Father had been so thoughtful. We kept the dog, and a year later Freddy made money by selling her puppies.

Father had married Mother with hopes for their bright future, and now sometimes she would curse him this way or say she did not love him anymore. Sometimes she would tell us all that she had nothing to live for. I have an early vision of her in the kitchen, by the stove, screaming at us to leave the house so she could gas herself. I was terrified that Father would herd us out and let Mother put her head in the oven. He knew she would apologize for her behavior when she felt better, but still he had to listen to the woman he loved say she did not love him or their children or the home that he had made as a haven for her. Whole and well, she adored him. Manic, she could not keep her hands off him. Depressed, she seemed to loathe him and all he did.

We never had time to heal from one episode to the next. She would tear our souls, and when we thought the house was safe again, there she would go. Whether her illness made her say threatening and menacing things or not, Father did not want to hear that she did not love him. And of course, neither did Freddy and I. It was hard to keep in mind that she was only mouthing words she could not help but say. I had to work at reminding myself. So did my father. My first memory of language, at four, is of his voice. It is bedtime and he is in the bathroom with her. He is asking Mother to take words back, all the way back.

II

Nine

I have always believed two days in June of 1963 to be emblematic of my family's life then, our entire world in miniature. It was as though we became hung in time, so that our problems and frustrations would play themselves out, so that we could see Mother both sick and well, feeble and strong, comprehensible and enigmatic. I experienced such an avalanche of unaccustomed ideas and sensations that I would be years sorting through the rubble, wondering at how much my life was showing me and how much I was expected to retain. And it was the first time I came to understand my brother, to see him as a member of what we were trying, that weekend, to pass off as a family. Before, he seemed separate and apart from our parents, with no need for the kind of maternal attention I was hungering for. We treated him, and he treated himself, like a boarder. But he surprised me. I discovered that he and I had the same agenda. He was the sort of boy who would have ridiculed Tiny Tim for walking funny, so I am not surprised that my earliest clear, sustained, and wholly reliable memory of him starts on the first of those two days, with his laughing at me while I vomited over the second-story balcony of what I recall as Mr. Barnes's magnificently ramshackle beach house.

Except in sheer size, the house was not impressive. It was three-storied and on stilts, with a cupola, a widow's walk, two stoves, two refrigerators, and everybody's cast-off sofas, armchairs, and rugs. All the rooms were pine-paneled, dented here and there over the years by grandchildren who on rainy days had ridden tricycles and red toy tractors into the walls. The kitchen table, covered in red-and-white-checkered oilcloth, was made of three doors buttressed underneath by sawhorses and joined at right angles to form a U. There were four bedrooms, one for the maids and cooks, one for Mr. Barnes, two others for his sons and their wives. Younger children slept on pull-out sofas in their parents' rooms. Older ones were relegated to the sleeping balcony that ran the length of the house and caught every breeze and sound from the shore.

Mr. Barnes was never concerned that the house or furnishings be first-rate. Raised so poor that he could see stars through the cracks in the boards above the bed he shared with his two brothers, he was living out his childhood fantasy of having a beach house even though owning beach property was the province of moneyed city-dwellers. On vacation, his neighbors were professional men with whom he had little in common other than an interest in investments. While other men dressed in casual clothes—Bermuda shorts and Ban-Lon tops—Mr. Barnes walked the strand in gray pants and a starched white shirt, which he changed two or three times a day, creating an enormous amount of vacation laundry for Pearl or Aunt Menefee's maid, whoever was on duty at the time. The shirts had to be washed, soaked in Argo starch, rolled in plastic wrap, and refrigerated overnight, dried, sprinkled with water, and ironed the next day. My mother encouraged him to dress more appropriately and lured him into men's departments to show him open-necked knit shirts when he took her shopping, but he would not surrender his starched ones. He finally did capitulate with the shoes, changing from brown leather lace-up wingtips to canvas slip-ons. He continued, however, to wear dark socks, telling my father that only a man with a foot fungus should wear white.

I never heard of him inviting his Nash County neighbors to the beach house. He let them conjure their own visions of its grandeur. The wives of farmers who lived on either side of him at home must have watched my grandmother and then him loading the car for a beach trip when all they had to look forward to in the summers was canning peaches and chopping cotton. If they went anywhere, it was to White Lake, where they would sweat in shotgun shacks and perhaps spring for the fifty-cent ride on the glass-bottomed boat, only to look down between their feet and see mud. They would not watch distant ships from a cupola, and they would not enjoy a light wind on a long balcony. They would not sit around a table with mounds of boiled shrimp on a newspaper, peeling them, dipping them in melted butter.

Mr. Barnes thought I was still too young, even at eight, to sleep on the balcony. On the afternoon that I vomited I was supposed to be resting in bed beside my Sominexed mother, guarding her, so Father could enjoy a few minutes of surf-casting with Uncle Lawrence. Pearl and Olive could not guard her, as they were taking a few days off with their family at Carolina Beach, a place I never heard called anything except "the colored beach." Mother had awakened us that morning with the news that she meant to jump off Mercer's fishing pier. She had not been "right," as Pearl would have said, when we left home, and she got only worse on the way to the coast. Father kept telling her that she would feel better once she was with Mr. Barnes.

"He always makes you more cheerful, Maggie," Father said.

I knew Mr. Barnes did not, not always. He had not healed her. Mother turned to the window and fogged it up with her despairing sobs. Freddy sighed with a combination of adult resignation and adolescent petulance. He knew we were in for a long trip. And with no Pearl. I did hope Mr. Barnes could help Mother, as I could not see how she could become any sadder.

"What're you crying about, honey?" Father put his hand on her shoulder.

She pushed his hand away, twisted more

into the car door, and said, "I don't know. I honestly don't know."

At least I knew it was not something I had done. I had seen her cry over nothing enough times to know that she needed no catalyst. While I would blame myself for her mood swings other times, that day I did not. I relaxed a little, relieved that I did not have to process any guilt. Freddy was seething, though. He was trying to read one of his Modern Library editions of something, and every now and then he would close the book and sigh again in despair over being trapped in the car with her. He once told me he remembered that trip well, remembered thinking that he would have preferred having both Mother and Father roll up the windows and chain-smoke to the sound of Mother's incessant crying. "You couldn't read with all that going on," he said. You could not do much of anything while she cried except wonder how to make it stop. Many years later, when both my children were colicky and could not help but cry, I would have the same feeling of frustration, of not knowing how to make it stop. Had she not been my mother, had they not been my children, perhaps I could have turned down the volume.

I was not able to rest in the bed beside her,

either, nagged as I was by the noise of children playing out on the beach, children who had not been made to "come in out of the heat of the day" by their grandfathers. After Freddy and I learned that we would have to wait a couple of hours to be set loose outside, he told Father it was unfair.

"What's unfair," Father responded impatiently, "is children in Calcutta living in drainage pipes."

Freddy refused to acknowledge any relevance of Father's exasperated observation. He had heard it so many times before. When Father told him to find a quiet place and read a book, Freddy stalked out of the bedroom. Father kissed me on the forehead and told me to shout from the balcony if Mother woke up. He could tell that I was not comfortable with my responsibility. Freddy had openly refused to guard her, and Father did not make him. He assured me that she would be out for at least an hour. After Mother's death, when Father voiced regret about his recklessness in doping her up with an over-the-counter medication, he said, "But boy, would those things knock her out. Bam." Back then, I did not trust her to stay out for an hour. I believed she would awaken the minute he left the house, and wonder why I was there. She would turn to me and ask, "And why are you here?" I would not have been able to tell her. Then I would have to run to the balcony and shout out loud for my father, as though I were announcing the sudden sight of billowing smoke.

Instead of lying there worried looking at Mother, I slipped outside to the balcony with my life-sized doll Lou Effie to wait until one of Aunt Menefee's three-year-old twins awakened from the sort of drooling, stuporous afternoon naps that children seem to have only at the beach when the windows are wide open and floor fans are angled on them, or during feverish, codeine-laced night sweats of strep throat or measles. While I played with Lou Effie, I looked down on but did not disturb Mr. Barnes as he sat on the porch swing, reading *The Coastal Times*, an afternoon newspaper that called itself "the best mullet wrap money can buy." He had on a fresh white shirt, and he rocked slowly, back and forth, back and forth, just like those waves coming in and going out. The very words in my head were, "They match." The ocean whooshed and the swing squeaked in perfect time, and I observed and heard this matching business while I undressed and dressed Lou Effie. Then I grew clammy and weak, and then I felt lunch rising in my throat. I had just enough time to get to the railing. Because a barrier of chicken wire ran from the top of the railing to the roof, I had to press my lips to some of the rusty fencing and vomit in a way that made a natural and involuntary human function even more humiliating than it needed to be. The chicken wire was up because, as a toddler, my cousin Marshall had once fallen off the balcony and cracked his collarbone.

I would not have vomited on the balcony floor, because I was a fastidious child, and I knew I had no time to run all the way through the adjacent bedroom to the bathroom. Aunt Menefee might have caught me hunched over on all fours, like a sick puppy, ruining the carpet. My goal was to overshoot the porch, sending my lunch out onto the sand, where it would not bother anybody, particularly Mr. Barnes, who witnessed my troubles from about twelve feet below, but I could not manage this objective. Analyzing the situation from an adult, medical perspective, Freddy and I have agreed that only patients in the final, hideous stages of bubonic plague and boy babies with pyloric stenosis have ever been capable of the force that I would have needed to propel my peanut butter and jelly out onto the sand and sea oats. My blood pressure must have been negligible, because I also remember thinking that if I did not hold myself up by both hands on the chicken wire, I would fall down on the floor and die. And then Freddy arrived to jeer at me in my cotton panties and now streaked T-shirt.

Mr. Barnes threw his newspaper to the side, trotted down the steps, and walked backward a few paces until he could see what was happening on his balcony.

He shouted at Freddy, "Be quiet, you goddamn bully! Go get Miss Woodward and tell her to help Hattie, and then you come see me!"

Freddy stopped laughing at once, knowing he was about to be reprimanded by a professional.

As Freddy left the balcony, he hissed that he would pay me back. Although at the time I certainly had no knowledge of his rejection of me as an infant, or the bassinet-kicking episodes, I feared that the payback would entail his twisting my arm behind my back or pressing my fingers toward the tops of my hands until he was satisfied I had been punished enough. He was large for a fourteen-year-old, already taller than both our father and Mr. Barnes, and broader across the shoulders. He was well on his way to manhood, with the frequent outbreaks on his face and his teasing of

me two of the few remaining vestiges of ado-
lescence. More and more each day, he wanted
to be treated like a man, given man-sized por-
tions at dinner, allowed to practice driving the
car down the path with Hubert watching him
from the backseat. I knew, even then, that he
was thinking of himself as a young man, not
as an older boy. Freddy had big plans for himself, and he knew that his intelligence would
take him wherever he wanted to go. But still,
on that afternoon at the beach, he was a little
boy again, a bully.

There were cots at either end of the balcony,
and I got myself to one, lay down, and waited
for Miss Woodward, who had come to the
beach at Mr. Barnes's insistence. They were
just beginning to spend time together, although my grandmother had been dead for
nine years. Miss Woodward had recently
moved back from Kentucky, where she had re-
tired from being an elementary school teacher.
I remember wondering if Mother was ever
jealous of Miss Woodward and the time we all
knew she was spending with Mr. Barnes.
Mother had been the only woman in his life
since his wife's death. Now I know that
Mother was ambivalent. She would phone Mr.
Barnes's house to ask him to take her to town,
only to be told by the maid that he was al-

ready there with Miss Woodward. Pearl told me that Mother would confide in her after these calls, telling her, "I know it's for the best." And then, Pearl said, Mother would go about her day preoccupied by her exclusion.

So far, Miss Woodward had been entertaining my cousins and me, taking us on early-morning shell hunts, inspiring us to put together those sorts of thousand-piece covered-bridge puzzles that had not been touched in years, and in the main, acting as nursery maid and governess. I remember how she mastered Monopoly by reading the rules on the inside of the box and how she made the older children play with the younger ones and act happy about it. She also told my father and uncle all the things a man who wants to be left alone for the afternoon wants to hear, like, "Let me fix you a nice snack," or "Let me see if I can find an extra pillow," or "I don't see why you shouldn't just go to sleep right here."

Although Mr. Barnes had invited her for his companionship, not to tote and fetch for others, he did not rescue her from the roles of chatelaine and nursery maid. Perhaps he was proud that she did not choke at the bit, as did Aunt Menefee, who, even on vacation, was always a buzzing, vibrating wad of anxiety. She had nothing to do, especially now that her children were being tended by Miss Woodward, whose company they seemed to prefer. While my mother was ambivalent about Miss Woodward's role in our lives, Aunt Menefee interpreted her actions as part of a planned assault on the family, a ruse that men and children were too naive and gullible to see. Miss Woodward intended to alienate my grandfather's affections as a means of tricking him into marriage and moving into the big house, where she would fire the old cook, Julie, and install herself in the wonderful kitchen with the brick oven that had baked every loaf of bread Mr. Barnes had eaten for the past forty years. The thought of Miss Woodward in that kitchen, feeding Mr. Barnes, was probably even more repugnant to Aunt Menefee than the thought of these two old people sleeping together and seeing each other naked. The notion that he might miss the company of a sweet woman or that he saw his late wife in Miss Woodward's eyes was anathema to her.

I looked forward to the appearance of a gentle, white-haired Monopoly wizard beside my cot; I pretended as I lay there that Miss Woodward was actually my mother. I thought, This may be what it's like to have a mother. I imagined that something romantic like a vague fever had taken my mother and that I had gone to live with Miss Woodward. Although she was old enough to be a grandmother figure, and I could have used one of those also at that moment, I skipped directly to mother figure. I imagined that she hummed while she baked and crocheted. She had no life outside her altruism. She would take me in. Mr. Barnes would visit and show me a completely different face from the one he showed to the rest of the world. He would be a gentle man.

The door to my mother's bedroom was wide open, but she was still dead asleep. I was not angry that she was unavailable to me at a time when even the most inattentive mothers are supposed to take a temperature and apply a cool compress. I was relieved that she was still out. She was like an unruly child who is manageable only when asleep. She aroused pity in anybody who loved her, and by age eight, I could determine who loved her and who did not. So far, the list included only Mr. Barnes, Pearl, my father, Olive, Miss Woodward, Uncle Lawrence, and me on the favorable side. One of the reasons I knew Miss Woodward cared about her was that whenever she heard my mother was having one of her "spells," she sent over hand-rolled chocolate and coconut candies for Freddy and me. Also, she sent casseroles to Pearl. Using the recipes in *South-*

ern Living, she introduced the concept of the casserole in the Bend of the River community.

As for Freddy, I interpreted his sarcasm, his slights, and his whispered desires that Mother would vanish as signs that he hated her. In fact, several times when she was wandering the upstairs hall at home in her bathrobe, I was afraid my brother would sneak out of that room with all his nasty homemade "Keep Out" signs on the door and cause her to tumble down the steps. I saw how easily he could stick his foot out at the top of the staircase. When Freddy walked by her sleeping body that day, on his way to find Miss Woodward for me and punishment for himself, his mind must have been quick with "If it weren't for yous." He was probably saying to himself, "If it weren't for you being passed out, you would have heard Hattie out there and tended to her. If it weren't for you, Father and I could go fishing off the pier, but no, he's got to stay around in case you wake up and decide to do something. If it weren't for you, maybe I could have invited a friend down here with me. If it weren't for you, the old man wouldn't be waiting for me."

Miss Woodward arrived on the balcony, led me into the bedroom, and placed me beside my mother, telling me that I was slight and

that the rest of my cousins looked corn-fed.
Although she had no children, she did all the
things Pearl, who was also childless, did when
I was sick. She said I felt hot enough for aspirin, and then she examined the texture and
hardness of my fingernails. She joked that because she could think of no other way to di-
agnose me, she was now checking me as she
would a hen that refused to lay. Then she
shook Mother gently back into the world and
told her to pull herself together because I
needed her.

"Maggie," she said, "Hattie's sick. I'm sending out for crackers and ginger ale, and I want
you to help change her clothes and see if you
think the doctor needs to be called. Sit up now,
Maggie. Mr. Barnes can be here in a minute,
or I can get Frederick. Which one?"

Mother seemed oblivious to my presence,
too concentrated on dragging herself back
from wherever Father had sent her. When she
finally sat up, she moaned, "I don't care." She
stood and moved toward the bathroom.

I lay where she had been. The heat rising
from the mattress made me sick again, and
this time I ran to the bathroom, passing
Mother. On the way I heard Miss Woodward
repeating to my mother that she really should
look after me. I thought, Doesn't Miss Wood-

ward know that Mother is never the one who looks after me?

My mother told her, "Josephine, just let me get my feet under me. I'm real dizzy. Help me get on into the bathroom."

Miss Woodward held her by the arm and walked her the rest of the way, and then she went downstairs to find my father. She was back in a minute.

Until that day, I had never heard Miss Woodward's first name. I had never considered the idea that she might have one. When I was through vomiting, I sat on the bathroom floor with my head resting on the toilet seat and tried to figure out why my mother got to call Miss Woodward Josephine. Not even Mr. Barnes, who had authority and permission to do all things, called her anything other than Miss Woodward. Both she and Mr. Barnes were of a time when properly raised Southerners equated informality of address with being common, with going to the door in stocking feet or talking about one's gout at the table. Because I did not yet know my mother well enough to assign an indisputable motive to her, I was unsure if her informality signaled welcome familiarity or disrespect. I was too sick to cobble together anything other than the temporary explanations that allowances were made for Mother because she had mental problems and was Mr. Barnes's pet.

When Mother finally appeared at the bathroom door, she asked if I could move over a minute. She was pale. She said that hearing me had made her sick also. Miss Woodward pushed past her and somehow organized my body in a limply folded manner over the tub, and then helped my mother to her knees at the toilet. She told her she would feel so much better when this was over. My mother and I listened to each other's sickness, and when my father came to the door with a bottle of Emetrol, Miss Woodward spoke to him sharply.

"Where in God's name have you been, Frederick?"

She was all of a sudden tough. I did not know she was capable of this. She had a first name and she could curse. My immediate thought was that she might have learned it from Mr. Barnes. Maybe he was teaching her how he liked his sons talked to, and she was trying out her new voice on my father. The only other woman I had ever heard curse was my mother, and then only when she was cycling. Because of my mother's illness, my father knew how to tolerate a profane woman, and so he seemed immune to Miss Woodward's tone. He ignored her and opened the brown bottle of Emetrol. She left the room, and I heard her go downstairs.

Mother sat up and leaned against the wall, which was papered with what I believed to be Frenchy-looking combs, brushes, and mirrors. She closed her eyes.

"Frederick," she moaned, "this room is really spinning. Do not tell me you've been fishing while we've been up here dying." She sounded pleasant in comparison with Miss Woodward.

Father gave me and then Mother a teaspoon of the Emetrol, and as he put the spoon in her mouth, he whispered to her.

"I've been with Freddy, Maggie."

"What's wrong with Freddy?" Mother asked.

"Father slapped him."

"Over what?"

"Making fun of Hattie."

Mother scowled at me and then looked back at my father. "Is he okay?"

"No. I heard him outside, between the cars, crying. Everybody heard him, and when Lawrence and I went outside to see what was going on, we met Father coming up the back steps. He told me Freddy had been insolent, and when I asked about what, he told me that he had laughed at Hattie. I would have brought him up here, but the way you were this morning, I didn't know if you were able, and then Menefee stuck the Emetrol and a spoon in my hand. This is all a mess, Maggie. A real mess."

We heard loud voices from downstairs. Father went below to see what was going on. When he came back, he did not seem encouraged.

Mother asked him what the noise was all about.

He said he had seen Miss Woodward at the bottom of the stairs, talking to Mr. Barnes. All of a sudden Mr. Barnes grabbed her and struck out walking toward the Bald Head Island ferry. "Lawrence ran out there and tried to stop him. You can imagine what little good that did."

"Where's Freddy?" Mother asked.

Father said he was with Aunt Menefee in the other bedroom.

"Bring him to me right now," Mother ordered.

She splashed water on her face and helped me into a clean top and shorts. I was feeling much better, as though the peanut butter and jelly had been a poison in my system that had needed to come out. Looking back, I think I might have had a twenty-four-hour bug.

Mother and I sat on the bed and waited for Father and Freddy. I tried, unsuccessfully, to think up something to say to her. She had never, that I could recall, dressed me. I could have thanked her for that, for now finally touching my body. Her face had changed. Before, she had looked flat. Now she was alive, alert, ready for her first patient to walk into the examining room. Even though I had no experience with her protecting me, I moved closer to her, because I was afraid of how Freddy would look, and also because I was afraid he would somehow "get me" for having caused Mr. Barnes to "get him." I was responsible for all this, I thought. I should have vomited in the bathroom, or on the bedroom floor for that matter, and let Freddy mock me as he pleased, out of Mr. Barnes's range of hearing.

Freddy came in behind Father, and when they were both inside, he ran to lock himself in the bathroom. Although he was in fast motion, I could see that his cheek was still a mottled red. I remember thinking how big he was to have been slapped. I did not understand the full meanings of the words "degraded" and "humiliated," but that must have been how Freddy felt to have Mr. Barnes slap him in the face over so small a sin as teasing a little sister.

Ten

My next memory of that weekend is of lying down on a cot on the balcony. Mother put a summer blanket over me and told me to call out if I needed anything. I knew better than to need anything. She had plenty to do. She had to be a parent to Freddy, and that was quite the limit of her capacity. If I needed anything, I decided, I would call my father. Later, in the full moonlight, I could see my parents asleep in the double bed. Mother was sprawled sideways. Father had a thin sliver of space, and I was afraid he would fall off and hit his head on the night table. Freddy was asleep on the pull-out sofa, with a blanket completely covering his head.

I had as little luck resting then as I had had that afternoon; so many things were on my mind. I got out my art supplies and sat on the balcony floor and made Freddy a heart. I told him that I loved him and I was sorry I was sick. If I had known this then, I would have written that I suspected he had been slapped because I was Maggie's baby, and that Mr. Barnes had been bound by his nature to strike out against any unsavory trait that he suspected he shared with his grandson. When he caught Freddy being a bully, he was looking at his own reflection. My only other sensation was a grinding hunger. Because of all the commotion with Miss Woodward's setting out for Bald Head, I had not been served the promised ginger ale and crackers. I tiptoed to the bathroom and put my mouth under the faucet and drank until I felt full.

When my parents woke up, they did not think I was awake, and I saw my mother carefully move the covers from around Freddy's face and then frown, peeking at his eye the way a grandmother would make a little tent over a newborn's legs to check for plumb lines. She kept the covers down, and I saw that he had a bright welt on his cheek. She looked at me and said suddenly, "I forgot to feed you," and then started crying.

Father offered to drive to the beach house Pearl was sharing with her sister from Jonesboro and bring Pearl and Olive back with him, but Mother was adamant that Pearl not be collected until absolutely necessary. I think she was afraid for her to see Freddy's face. She may have been worried that Pearl would ask what she intended to do about it, what retribution she had planned, and there would have been no answer. My mother had not yet spoken of "getting" Mr. Barnes, but I assumed that she would. Although I had never seen her protecting Freddy from anything, I thought that the circumstances were enough for even *her* mothering instincts to kick in. And although Freddy had merely teased me, even though he had been slapped in the face and not whipped with a belt or a coat hanger or whatever else Mr. Barnes could have put his hands on, I believed that he deserved protection and that Mr. Barnes deserved retaliation. I remember thinking, You do not hit other people's children. My father's reasons for not confronting him were obvious, but my mother knew that she stood no chance of being hit or castigated.

Whenever I hear an airline stewardess advise passengers to secure the emergency oxygen masks on themselves before they assist small children, I think of my mother on that morning. The airline advice runs contrary to every emotion a mother has when a child is in trouble, but in Mother's case, she knew that if she could not breathe, neither could Freddy. Father told me once, when one of my daughters was being a little pill at Thanksgiving and I told her I was tempted to spank her, that I should not threaten this punishment. "Your mother and I," he said, "agreed never to hit our children. I took too many whippings coming up. That's one of the reasons Father's slapping Freddy caused me such anguish. He had interfered with my promise to your mother. It was typical of him."

Mother must have assumed that Mr. Barnes and Miss Woodward had come back from Bald Head, and she must have believed that Miss Woodward would be downstairs closing ranks, insofar as one person can close ranks, around Mr. Barnes. So Miss Woodward would not be of any assistance, and I was certainly of no use. Aunt Menefee was out of the question. She had her own problems, or as my mother would have said, her own set of problems. So Mother had only herself to depend on.

Mother's crying awakened Freddy. We could all smell bacon frying downstairs. He asked if we had already eaten. Father told him we had not gone downstairs yet, although he planned to get dressed and bring a tray up for Mother. I knew he did not want Aunt Menefee to see her in tears and start with all the questions she could not help but ask. She always wanted to know what had happened to make Mother so upset. Father once remarked that he felt foolish telling her that nothing had happened and that any other nearly true answer he gave was never good enough. Aunt Menefee always wanted to know more. Father told Freddy he could have anything he wanted for breakfast. He would tell the cook to fix Freddy a plate when he went downstairs after Mother's. But Freddy said he was not hungry. I knew he was, but he feared the aftershock that might occur if Mr. Barnes found out he had pleased himself with an unrepentant serving of ham and eggs.

Although Freddy was the first grandchild I knew to be hit by Mr. Barnes, it was not difficult to extrapolate the old man's expectations; Freddy was to realize that the blow itself completed his grandfather's direct role and now he had to assume the responsibility of punishing himself more, until even the tiniest

impulse to repeat the offense was routed and
destroyed. Also, if he had been able to go
downstairs that morning, Aunt Menefee
would have sniffed his wound. She would
have detected his vulnerability and fallen on
him the way sharks feed on their injured fel-
lows. She would have found some subtle way
to show Mr. Barnes whose side she was on,
falling in line with Miss Woodward even
though Aunt Menefee spent her time exclud-
ing her, gossiping about people she knew
nothing about, leaving her no inroad, no pas-
sage into the family circle, talking about Mr.
Barnes's late wife as if Miss Woodward were
threatening competition and my aunt were a
schoolgirl come to defend a cheerleader's boy-
friend against the threat of an interloper.

My mother took the problem of Freddy's
contrition and turned it over and around in
her head like an object, a lacquered box or a
porcelain vase worth a great deal or perhaps
nothing at all. She quickly decided that Freddy's breakfast was valuable enough to lie for.

"Frederick," she said, "go downstairs and
tell your father I'm sick. Say I feel so rotten I
can hardly breathe, but be sure to emphasize
that I don't want him to see me quite yet. Tell
him what I really want is a nice tray made up,
and then you bring that to Freddy. I'm actu-

ally not hungry. If anybody asks how Freddy is, say he's okay. Say he's baby-sitting Hattie."

Freddy protested, because he was afraid to be caught eating. "Suppose he comes in here anyway?" he asked.

"He won't, son. Get your robe on, Frederick. Go ahead."

My father kissed her on the cheek in gratitude, and in perfect astonishment that she would defy Mr. Barnes to comfort a son who rolled his eyes and sighed like a world-weary cynic whenever she spoke to him and who sleepily dismissed everything she said because she was confined to the house so much of the time and was therefore ubiquitously clueless.

When Father left the room, I crawled onto the bed with Mother. She looked at me sideways, as if she were a gull beside which some other bird had landed. When I looked at Freddy's face, he shut his eyes and lifted his chin the way a haughty woman does when she decides that a conversation is over. No one spoke. Father soon bumped the door open with a tray.

"Is it safe for Freddy to eat?" Mother asked.

"He's not here, Maggie," Father answered. "Miss Woodward isn't either. They never came back from Bald Head. It's really awful downstairs. Lawrence, poor bastard, had saved today to drive to Fort Fisher to see the new Civil War exhibit, and Menefee's got him out there loading the car as fast as she can throw suitcases at him."

"You mean they left and never came back."

"Yes, Maggie."

"You mean they did not sleep in their beds."

"Yes."

"You mean they just left."

"Now Maggie, I've said it three times."

"Well, what are you going to do?"

"Why am I supposed to do anything? Or should I?" Clearly, Father needed her help.

"What would he do if he were you?" she said.

So my father's job was not to figure out what he himself would do as much as it was to decide what Mr. Barnes would do if one of his sons had slapped a child in the face hard enough to bruise him and then retreated in hurricane season with a woman not his wife to an island that had no phone service. He had to set Mr. Barnes in motion, watch him, follow him, and listen to him. Then he would plot a matching course. I wonder how much time my father spent hoping his father would do the right thing so that he could do it, too. Very simply, he had to see all the apparent possibilities. My father had to consider what his father would have done, and then he had to prophesy the consequences of his actions.

If Mr. Barnes did not care one way or the other what two reasonable people did with or to each other on their vacation, he would have left them alone. If, however, he did care, he would march across the ocean, collect them, and box their ears on the homeward-bound ferry. Father must have seen himself catching the next ferry, combing the tiny island for my grandfather and Miss Woodward, and finding them enjoying breakfast at one of the few habitations then on the island, a cottage owned by Mr. Cheshire, one of Mr. Barnes's few close friends. I cannot picture Mr. Barnes running into the cottage, confessing that he had escaped to Bald Head because he had humiliated his grandson. No, I bet that he acted as if this was old times with his friend.

And then here would come my father to spoil the reunion. He would enter the door with his straw hat in his hands, and greet the Cheshires as though he had just stepped into a funeral parlor. He would sound doleful when he inquired after their health. Then he would go over to the table and relate the family's fear that Mr. Barnes and Miss Woodward had drowned, and my grandfather would know that the real fear was Aunt Menefee's vision of him and Miss Woodward shacked up for the night in a creaky bed with sandy sheets. About the time my father would open his mouth to say when the next ferry departed, he would be backhanded across Mrs. Cheshire's kitchen. He would lie there sprawled, with his hand to the edge of his mouth, like a cowboy in a barroom fracas. And so my father stayed put.

But somebody downstairs was doing a lot of something. I could hear a great banging of pots and pans, doors slamming, children crying, all sounds of a rapid evacuation. I could hardly believe I was big enough to have started such a cataclysm, but I had. Uncle Lawrence was being sent scrambling underneath beds to look for stray tennis shoes while Aunt Menefee stood at the door barking her next orders, which, I heard her yell, were to rinse sand off the beach toys and to tie bags to the top of the car. Uncle Lawrence would have gone right to work, knowing that as he sprayed and strapped he would be assaulted with the news of what a sloppy job he had done. I remember feeling especially sorry for him because of his dashed plans to visit Fort Fisher. He had the look of a man who never gets to go anywhere, whose idea of cutting loose becomes two hours at a matinee movie with a tub of popcorn all his own.

Aunt Menefee's maid and cook did everything at one speed, and Pearl said it was maddening to watch them. Somehow, though, they always got things done on time. But Aunt Menefee must have been driven completely 'round the bend watching those two women wash breakfast dishes, slumped over with their elbows on the sink, slowly rinsing one side of a plate and then the other, staring at the bottom of a dirty frying pan, wishing they had kept a sharper eye on the eggs, casually discussing their church involvements and rheumatoid ailments as if checkout were sometime later than as soon as humanly possible. The fact that neither the maid nor the cook got fired proves only that Aunt Menefee was not premenstrual.

One of her chief anxieties was the fact that she was, at that moment, losing what little control of Mr. Barnes she possessed. She ordered his meals each week, paid Julie, paid his housekeeper, checked her work, and gave her little projects when she ran out of things to do in a ten-room house with a sole male tenant who considered it ill-mannered for a person to leave any sort of trail, whether it be dirty socks or bread crumbs. To lose day-to-day contact with a man's laundry and food was to lose the man, and since Aunt Menefee had lost Uncle Lawrence's love and respect almost the minute he had been acquired, she hopped on Mr. Barnes as soon as my grandmother died, running whatever part of his life he would allow to be run, until the moment he took off with Miss Woodward. Somewhere on that island, that's who had folded his white shirt across a chair so it would look as neat as he liked it in the morning. That's who was reassuring him that his hair looked fine combed back just with his fingers. That's who was asking if he was hungry while she turned sand out of his cuffs.

And was she promising to marry him, too? This Aunt Menefee would have found particularly revolting. She discounted the fact that Mr. Barnes and Miss Woodward were related only by marriage, and that his late wife might have been grateful to her sister for alleviating a pain that would have been evident to anybody who peeked through his window at midnight to see him tossing fitfully in a room that reeked of loneliness, a room still arranged as it had been the day she died, with her gray hair caught in her monogrammed brush and the last letter from her Chinese missionary friend out of its envelope, with pertinent passages underlined, as if she had been pondering a careful reply.

Aunt Menefee would have reached her conclusions as to what was going on at Bald Head without giving careful regard to the fact that Mr. Barnes was not the type of man either to seduce a woman or to allow himself to be seduced. And besides, he had just spent so much physical and spiritual energy on Freddy that probably all he wanted to do was lie down with his head in Miss Woodward's lap. They might have bundled, but I imagine nothing beyond a quiet holding. Looking back, I see Mr. Barnes as being quite prudish. Although "God damn" was ground in like a stain on his tongue, if his sons had been caught telling an off-color joke in the company of women, he would have flogged them; once, when discussing a bovine breeding problem with a veterinarian, my father heard him uncomfortably refer to a penis as "the male offering." He had puritanical ideas about the roles of men and women, saying, for example, that Mrs. Barnes could not write a check in public because the act was "mannish." He viewed check-writing by women to be almost as deleterious to the feminine ideal as voting, which Mrs. Barnes did not do, either. She always said that her husband knew the issues and that even if she stayed up all night praying for the wisdom to vote correctly, she was still not certain she would not become flabbergasted when presented with the names of all those strangers.

Aunt Menefee knew she would not be able to "act right" when Mr. Barnes returned, and acting right meant pretending she had not noticed that he and Miss Woodward had spent the night away. My aunt was afraid that he would walk in unannounced and catch her making beds, cursing pillowcases and fitted sheets that seemed alive in a demonic struggle to keep her from getting out of the house. She was the sort of woman who drives men to other women, and while there is no evidence that Uncle Lawrence did anything other than endure his lot dutifully, he was no doubt pinched, prodded, and jabbed underneath the table if he spoke to my mother for too long. Uncle Lawrence could have used a spot of time at the beach to appreciate the sight of my mother in her polished toenails and that polka-dot bathing suit she bought one manic summer, without dread of an up-all-night gnawing from Aunt Menefee about "exactly what Maggie has that I don't."

But Aunt Menefee was making them return home. Uncle Lawrence had been brought up better than to let a woman drive a car farther than to the beauty shop and back, and Rocky Mount was four hours away. He could not let his wife leave the beach alone any more than he could let her mow the grass or open her own car door. Mr. Barnes had trained him to believe that men who allowed their wives and children to take off on long car trips were asking for whatever the escaped convicts or flim-flam tire-changers did to them on the side of the road. Even if Uncle Lawrence maintained a gleeful, ongoing fantasy of slamming his wife's fingers in a car door, he would open it for her and take care that she did not get grease on her skirt.

Suddenly, Mr. Barnes's beach house was quiet. Their leave-taking lasted about an hour, and in no time during that hour did my father offer to descend the steps into the buzz saw. My father and my uncle talked briefly in the hall, and Father assured his brother that he understood why he and his family were leaving. Uncle Lawrence told Father that Mr. Barnes would come back mad and that we should go home, too.

"I don't want to be here when they get back any more than Menefee does," my father said. "He's bound to come in fuming. It's just a matter of when it happens. I'll go ahead and take mine now."

This completely confused me. Take his now for what? What had Father done? *Mr. Barnes* was supposed to be the one in trouble. I had been, but he had taken over from me. In fact, I thought that was why he had left. He was ashamed. But how could he be ashamed and come back and punish Father? If you were humiliated, you hid. If you were in the right, you stayed in the clearing. Mr. Barnes was all over the place, firing in all directions, disregarding rules about who won and who lost. And since I had officially started all this, what was I supposed to be doing? I did not know. I huddled against my mother. She had offered to protect Freddy by lying to Mr. Barnes, and now she could protect me from whatever might be coming my way. If Mr. Barnes blew back in the door with the intention of directing the canister shot at us, I wanted her to shield me. His shame, recast as hostility, would have been awful to witness.

"Frederick," Mother said, "we'll just go on about our business. If you need to go to the grocery, then leave, and you can go ahead and get Pearl and Olive, I guess. I still dread what Pearl will say about Freddy's face, but I need her here anyway. I'm really feeling as though I didn't sleep well."

That was an ominous statement. If Mother announced she had not slept well, it meant her thoughts were starting to skid about rudderless. By evening, she might be going through every *Reader's Digest* in the house, laughing wildly at tedious anecdotes, quizzing herself on word-builder exercises, demanding that my father play along. I do not remember her biting her nails or tapping anything, but sometimes her speediness, with no outward clue, signaled danger ahead. She had undergone so much stress with the interrupted bout of depression the previous day, the self-willed cessation of her tears, the spectacle of the cheek, and now, after having carried her this far, her mind could have been announcing that it had just about had enough.

Father dressed to go get Pearl and Olive, and Mother went downstairs to check on things. While she was out of the room, I gave Freddy his card. He thanked me, but barely, and then he was quiet again. He could have shredded the card. He could have blared that he did not want to touch anything I had made, but he did not rip the card or attack me for having made it, because that would not have furthered his cause, which was to forget what had happened to him. I think he was still too shocked over Mr. Barnes's apparent inability to restrain his temper to do much besides stay in our parents' bedroom and wait for some feeling of being just a boy to return to him.

Eleven

We heard Father leave Mr. Barnes's house, but Mother did not come back upstairs. I hoped she was down there succeeding in her struggle to be well, going through all the motions indicative of sound mental health, seeing whether my yellow raft needed inflating, calling home to ask our family doctor if my nausea sounded like a little virus or something worse. He would ask her if I might have gotten hold of any bad shellfish. She would be insulted and say she would never serve anything older than that same day's catch to her family. I wanted her to open the utility room underneath the house, in between the stilts, to see if Aunt Menefee had left any decent sand toys for me. If she was down there meeting any disappointments, I wanted her to absorb them, then come back upstairs and tell Freddy and me that everything had been taken care of. We would be fine. We had food and games and books and the whole rest of the week without cousins. We would travel when Freddy felt up to it. That is how I wanted her to talk. I wanted her to be laughing-well, in her occasional state in which everything seemed to bring her joy. I wanted my father to bring back tomato soup, and I wanted her to fix it for me with toast crumbs scraped over the top. I did not want him to do this. I wanted my mother to do it.

She stayed downstairs for a long time. I hoped she was organizing herself, playing house until Pearl arrived to take over. I was rooting for her to be well enough to confront Mr. Barnes when he returned from Bald Head. I imagined her asking him what had been on his mind. She could say to him, "Didn't you realize that when you slapped my son, you slapped me?"

Freddy and I went out onto the balcony. The strand was full of families. I wanted so badly to be out of my T-shirt and panties and into my bathing suit, and I prayed that later in the

160

afternoon I would be out there on the water's edge with all those other children, who had not spent as bizarre a day as I had. Freddy stood at the railing and hooked his fingers in the chicken wire, just as I had done the day before. He asked if I was feeling any better, and I told him I was. Then he wanted to know if I was as bored as he was. The answer was yes. He told me to go in the bedroom and find his checkerboard, and when I returned with it, he had me set the game up on the floor. He spoke with his back to me. I did what he said, and then he turned around and rested his elbows on the railing behind him. He told me that I was black and he was red and that he was going first. He moved the checkers around on the board with his big toe. I wanted to stand, as he was doing, because I liked the idea of playing checkers with my feet, but instead I sat cross-legged, facing the ocean, and tried not to make inane moves.

I heard the downstairs door open and slam, and then I stood up and saw my mother trotting out toward the ocean. She had not been playing house. She had been downstairs losing her mind again. Although I had heard her threaten to drown herself more than once, particularly when we were at the beach and near so much water, I believed her every time. Each new announcement caused me to visualize how it would occur. She would not wait until midnight, leave the house, and wade into a moonlit ocean. No, she would run into the waves in full daylight, dive in, and never come back up. She would run across the sand, just as she was doing now. I could not move. I told Freddy Mother was about to drown herself. I told him to stop her.

He looked out at her, and even though he yelled with such volume and pitch that the sound is still in my ears, she did not stop. She took a sharp turn to the left just as she reached the water's edge. We watched her. Was she choosing another point of entry? She kept going, and we kept watching, and in the distance we saw two people moving toward her in a deliberate way. They were not amblers on the beach merely headed in her direction. They were Mr. Barnes and Miss Woodward. As my mother got closer and closer to them, she waved, and when they all came together, my brother and I saw Mother and Mr. Barnes embrace, like the old friends they were. At the moment our mother's betrayal broke Freddy's spirit, he upset the checkerboard with his foot and ran to the bathroom, where I heard him crying loudly, not even muffling the sound with a towel.

The impetus that made Mr. Barnes strike Freddy was the same force, only inverted, that drew my mother to him. I figured that out when I returned home and played with a set of magnets I had won in the school science bee. I became fascinated by their contradictory behavior. Held one way, they rushed to collide, but if I turned one around, the effect was the opposite. As I tried to nudge them together, they quivered apart, without ever touching. That same year, I learned about the force of gravity in outer space, the principle of repulsion and attraction that keeps planets from banging into each other, but bound to each other as well. My mind leaped backward to the day Mother was pulled down that beach by love and fear, lured to Mr. Barnes like metal shavings sliding across the kitchen table toward my new magnet. I did not consider the fact that had she confronted Mr. Barnes, he might have turned on her for the first time, and because she had seen grown people withered by him, she wanted to avoid his obloquy. I believed she counted on him, maybe even more than on my father, to look after her, and she needed to stay within his sphere to assure herself of his availability.

I did not explain my theory to Freddy, who believed he had been abandoned. I did not talk to him, because I knew he would not have listened. He had his own theory about Mother and Mr. Barnes. He told me once that she should have married him instead of our father. If I had been able to talk to my mother, I might have put all the theories to rest. She could have told me about herself. But we did not have that sort of time together. I had such a backlog of things to say to her that picking one to start with seemed an insurmountable task. And I had never been given the opportunity. I can actually remember passing her wordlessly in the hallway of our home, moving over to the side so she could get by, as though we were two strangers on a narrow sidewalk.

III

Twelve

The more I thought about Duke, the more confident I felt that my mother would be sorted out and sent home the person I had known only in brief bursts of wellness. If she could be well all the time, then I could have girls over to play. They would see my room, something no child outside my family had yet done. Other children from school always rode the bus home together, giggling as they disembarked and talking about building forts in pine thickets, about listening to records and learning new dances. I never went to anyone's house. As much as Pearl did for me, she never thought it her place to call mothers and set up play times. I understand that she would have felt awkward. I told myself that I did not want to be inside anybody's perfect household, a place in such contrast to my own, but I did want to go home with the girl who was the first in my class to have a Barbie doll. I imagined all the other girls, sitting on the floor, squealing over Barbie. There was something missing in me, something that did not allow me to squeal, a joy lacking. When my father brought a Barbie from town after he had read a newspaper article about the phenomenon, I sat her on my shelf with my Madame Alexander dolls and gazed at her. Maybe those dolls represented my mother to me; I could be so near them, yet not handle them with the almost aggressive affection I wanted to give them. I did not join the Girl Scouts, because I knew my turn would come to host a meeting at my house, and there was no way to predict Mother's condition. I would get off the bus alone and go in the house to be fed a snack by Pearl, and if Mother was depressed or delusional, I would be told either not to make noise when I went upstairs or not to go upstairs at all.

Pearl would tell me, "Your mother had funny ideas in her head today. Maybe you ought to stay in the kitchen and work on your lessons." When Freddy arrived home later, he would be told the same things, but he never obeyed. If I needed help, I would persuade Pearl to let me go to Freddy's room, where he would check my homework, leading me one step further into a math problem, and saying that it was not enough to know states and capitals, I needed to know principal agricultural and industrial products as well. I had won the third-grade science bee because of his instruction to memorize all the answers to everything that could have possibly been asked. He advised me to think of grammar school science as a finite body of knowledge to be mastered. He drilled me nightly. He told me about Dr. Joyce Brothers's winning on *The $64,000 Question*, in the boxing category. He told me he had never missed a question on a test, not ever. Although he did not say we had to prove something to our teachers, that was exactly what we were doing. We were overcompensating. Also, he realized that superior grades would take him a lot farther from home than the shiny, newly minted coin sets that Mr. Barnes gave each of his grandchildren on Christmases and birthdays, with the warning that we would never see another one if he found out that the money had been spent on candy or other foolishness. "You save them, and watch them be worth something," he would command.

Freddy learned three languages the Berlitz way. I remember how Pearl would put her ear to his closed door while his language records were playing, how she would stop in the hall with her arms full of sheets and towels, saying nothing, but thinking, I am sure, what an odd soul was in there, bent over the record player he was always borrowing from me, repeating things she believed he would never say to a real human being, or at least not to one who would offer him employment. Freddy's maturity was inchoate, a hodgepodge of childhood innocence, adolescent confusion, and adult wisdom. Most of the time, Freddy was his brain, and when his brain was resting, he was arms and legs playing basketball, usually shooting free throws, with Hubert stationed off to the side to chase the rolling ball until it stopped at the fence. Pearl had always viewed Freddy's refusal to try out for the basketball team as a sign that he lacked ambition.

"He's so good with that ball," she once remarked as she stood at the kitchen window watching him. "See him out there? Count them. Twelve, thirteen, fourteen. He's got a touch. Look at Hubert scooting that ball back to him with the garden hoe."

I seemed to have nearly the same degree of academic promise as Freddy, but my intelligence was more acceptable to her. My grades were not gifts from above or, as Pearl feared, from below. Pearl simply did not understand Freddy's aptitude, because the practical applications were not apparent to her. I was a smart little girl who did her homework at the kitchen table while Pearl cooked dinner. I kept Pearl company when Olive was working in another part of the house, and I thanked her for after-school cookies and put my plate in the sink, whereas Freddy blew through the kitchen and grabbed all he could hold and scurried off to his room, like an ant carrying picnic crumbs.

What Pearl wanted was for him to be accessible to our family. He was not. If Mother had been well enough to look, she would have seen him and would have felt the wonder at having such a gifted son. She might have realized that the same essence of understanding and intellect that drove him to such academic heights were inextricably bound up with her manic depression, and if the maternal role in passing on the marked gene had been postulated at the time, she would have watched him for signs of the illness. She could have predicted his future for him. If Father had not been so preoccupied with getting things done, with keeping the household in some sort of order resembling a family, he would have patted Freddy on the back more, and even if the touch would have felt a bit like the approbation a dog would receive after fetching a stick, I think Freddy still would have been grateful for it.

I did not want to stay in my room while Mother was being taken away to the hospital. I did not want to watch from my window. Rather, I wanted to be with her up until the moment she left in the car. And so I fell in line behind the doctor, noting his baggy trousers, thin and shiny in the seat, and his jacket pockets, which I took to be stuffed with everything that might drop through the holes in his pants pockets. My family was one of the few in the county who ever paid the man in real money. His remuneration often came in jelly jars of camellias for his wife and paper bags of hardened leftover Christmas candy for his children. Heaven knows how much Mr. Barnes overpaid him for this house call to Mother's bedside and his subsequent ride to Duke to assure that she was checked in and recognized as a true emergency and a woman of some means by the attending physician. I remember I wished he were wearing a suit that was in keeping with his dignity and station. He carried his black bag under his arm and seemed very burdened with my mother's two leather suitcases. Hubert had not answered Father's call for help with the bags. I suspected he was asleep in the basement—a trick he sometimes pulled that Father had never caught on to.

We stopped at Pearl's room, and as Father knocked, I thought we might go through the house collecting people like Henny Penny, or the Bremen Town Musicians. Pearl opened the door but would not come out. She was still distraught over her culpability and could not seem to understand Father when he told her that letting Mother escape had turned out to be the best thing that could have happened. Pearl still cried. Olive sat in a straight wooden chair in the corner of Pearl's room and would not come out, either. She bayed like a trapped animal when she caught sight of my mother in the hall, her limp doll legs, her loose neck, her whole body kept upright only by the power in the arms of my father and Mr. Barnes. I thought they resembled two boys trying to manage an outsize doll like my floppy Lou Effie, trying to make her walk. I was afraid that Mother would twist her ankle or that one of them would step on her foot. I worried about her head, too, that they might accidentally bump her into the wall. I was worried, in fact, about every part of her, and I held my breath when Father stumbled momentarily on the edge of the carpet runner.

Mr. Barnes told Olive to hush and blow her nose and to go call the doctor's wife to say he might not be home that night, and then he and Father went to Freddy's room. Freddy would not come when Father knocked. He would not open the door. Mr. Barnes spoke to him.

"You better let me in, and I mean now, Goddamnit."

Freddy cracked the door and stuck his face out, as if he were an old woman who read the newspapers and was not so sure about this man who said that he had come to check her gas meter.

Mr. Barnes told Freddy that he was taking Mother to the hospital, and she wouldn't be back for some time, and while she was gone, he could straighten himself up.

"All I want you to do," he said, "is to get that chip off your goddamn shoulder. Now, tell her you'll do it."

Freddy regurgitated the words. "Good-bye, Mother. While you're gone, I'll get the chip off my goddamn shoulder."

When he slammed the door, the concussion caused my mother to lift her head and nearly achieve consciousness. Mr. Barnes seemed to be considering whether he should ask the doctor to hold his side of Mother while he went into Freddy's room and took off his belt, but he did not. He continued down the hall, and at the top of the steps he and my father discussed how to manage a curve with the dead weight of my mother. They sounded like the moving men who had struggled to deliver the new dresser and sleigh bed to Mother's room two weeks back, after she had gone on one of her spending sprees.

Freddy, I believed, would watch Mother's departure from his window, and when she was gone, would cry his fill and then go outside and infuriate Pearl by playing basketball as though nothing had happened. And he did these things. I see now that Pearl was wise, but her intuitive powers exceeded her ability to interpret behavior and assign motivations. She would not have noted the way Freddy played a violent, almost demented, game of horse against himself, snatching rebounds, flinging himself into the garage door, seeing how close he could come to breaking his collarbone or maybe slicing his elbow on the rusty door handle. I think he wanted to go to bed in pain that night. He would wonder how he might have changed the day's events by being a better boy.

I processed Mother's departure by locking myself in my room and straightening it thoroughly, obsessively. I separated my construction paper by color, rearranged the furniture of my dollhouse, put a deck of cards in order, and broke, at last, into tears over a missing joker.

I heard Pearl's door shut, and I heard her move through the hall and down the steps in her old slippers, which scrubbed the floor when she was too tired to pick her feet up. I assumed she was headed to the kitchen, where she would wonder how to remove the odor of cigarettes and spilled bourbon from the house, and contemplate what Father would like to eat when he returned from Duke that evening, if he returned at all. Maybe she was also considering all the men she had known, men married and unmarried who had tried to make time with her when she was twenty years younger and a hundred pounds lighter. She would run all these men through her mind, see their lying eyes, hear their glib voices, think about exactly what sort of rape artist a callous boy like Freddy Barnes could grow up to be.

While Pearl worried and Freddy nursed sore muscles in his room, I was in bed regarding my own room the way I often did, as a place where Mother rarely set foot. She had no idea what pictures I had on the walls, which large shells were filled with play jewelry Olive had given me for Christmas and which held erasers and paper clips, which friends' school pictures were pinned to my bulletin board in lieu of their actual presence in my room, which library books I had on my nightstand. I was thinking of Mother's new room, too. I saw her quiet in a hospital bed, squeezing my father's hand, feeling much better already.

Thirteen

I am glad that my youth spared me the knowledge of Mother's ordeal with electroconvulsive therapy. Freddy did not know what was happening to her, either. We were not to know for years, not until Father slipped during a telephone conversation with me. He was concerned about a new drug that had been prescribed for Mother, and he said, "I just want her to stay well. She couldn't bear any more of those treatments." I asked about the treatments, and he opened up to me in a flood of memory, after having kept the secret so long to himself. I phoned Freddy to ask if he had known. He was as surprised as I was. As residents dabbling in anesthesiology, we both had assisted in several electroconvulsive treatments. I thought back and put Mother in the place of my patients, as I am sure Freddy did.

She would have been hooked up to an IV and then injected first with atropine, a drug that dries oral secretions and prevents irregular heart rhythms. Next the anesthesiologist would have given her pentothal, and within seconds she would have been out. Then, to reduce the chance of vertebral fractures, he would have administered a muscle relaxant called succinylcholine. Her lower arm, below a tightened blood pressure cuff, would be the only place her convulsion could be seen. Her temples would have been washed with warm water and then smeared with an electrolytic conducting jelly. She would have been hooked up to EKG and EEG machines. A rubber gag would have been placed in her mouth, between her molars. Two assistants, probably male, would have pressed downward on her shoulders and thighs to prevent the jolt from dislocating her arms and legs as her doctor pushed a red button. There would have been a click. Approximately a hundred volts would have coursed through her for a little more than a second. When the current traveled through her slim body, the hand that had not received the relaxant would have turned red and curled back on itself, like foil Christmas wrapping in the fireplace. In three minutes she would have awakened on the thin rubber mattress, wasted and worn, like a stunned child whose parents were not looking and therefore did not run to yank her up out of the big wave that had knocked her over and would not allow her to regain her footing. Her doctor would have asked if she knew what had just happened to her. I needed for her to have known, but I also needed for her to have been so drugged that the violence of the act did not mangle her spirit. I wanted her to have told them to let her rest.

My father would have been waiting for her in her room. At first, he said, Mother could form only the dimmest, slightest picture of her family's faces. That inability to tap her memory was a side effect of the therapy. Once inside her, the electroconvulsive current worked like a hollow-point bullet, traveling a mysterious, riotous, and jagged path. The treatment let her forget her desire to talk nonstop for hours, but she also forgot the image of me on the first day of school; out goes the baby with the bathwater. Father had to coax her mind into accepting us all again. And like most of the ECT patients Father met at the hospital,

Mother suffered extreme frustration, knowing that temporary memory loss represented her share of the Faustian bargain made with the psychiatrist. I think of her mind as a meadow with one strip of grass pressed down in a heavily, habitually trodden manic-depressive course. The treatments were intended to make her lose her old way through the meadow, to give her mind time to heal, and the grass and wild flowers time to rise again so that when she looked at the field, all would appear to her uniform, level.

Father told me that after each treatment, he had to reacquaint her with Freddy and me by sitting beside her bed and showing her our school pictures from his wallet. Father told her about my report card, and about how I had been accused, unfairly, of plagiarism for using the word "distraught" in an essay on a D. H. Lawrence story called "The Rocking-Horse Winner," and how he had to write my teacher a note assuring her that I was not a cheater. This teacher had not had Freddy before me, so she had no idea that Mr. Barnes and my parents supplied us with an extensive array of magazines, novels, and encyclopedias and other reference books. Father told Mother that Freddy had enrolled in college-preparatory calculus classes at Wesleyan, on the other side of Rocky Mount, and that he was staying up to do his homework until three in the morning.

After one of the treatments, my father told me, Mother startled him with an honestly bewildered, drop-jawed stare when he offered to rinse the conducting jelly out of her hair, as he had done each Monday before. He had to explain who he was, and why he knew her well enough to wash her hair.

He gave her signposts: their playing bridge with the Farnhams the night before he enlisted; their honeymooning at the Homestead; her birthing Freddy in hundred-degree weather; Father's driving to antique auctions with the pony trailer hitched to the car because he always assumed, correctly, that something would be bought. He told her about my birth, how I wouldn't suck and how she then drank the lager. He told her about Pearl and Mr. Barnes and how it had always been a battle of wills, with each of them thinking, I know what is best for her. He told Mother she kept a mare at Mr. Barnes's stable.

"But it was Louisiana she remembered first," Father said to me. "She remembered how bright the sun was the day I got back to her. She was on a blanket, with her hair up in a red turban, broiling herself in the glare off the Quonset hut. All her friends were out there with her, lined up like hens on a big outdoor grill. She didn't have the family pram in Louisiana for Freddy, so she borrowed a wheelbarrow and made him a little bed with a tent. Very clever. Maggie remembered the wheelbarrow down to the rust spots. We talked about Louisiana all morning because that was all she could remember. She was so frustrated." She cried when she couldn't connect a face with Mr. Barnes's name, and Father kept no photograph of him.

Fourteen

Mother's treatments were given over an eight-week period, always before breakfast. After each one, when she felt stable enough to walk, Father would accompany her to the cafeteria, where she would eat ravenously. She gained twenty pounds in the hospital. Just as the rewiring of her circuitry made her forget the features of Mr. Barnes's face, it made her forget the absence of desire for food. I learned about her new size by overhearing Father's comments to Pearl. Later, Father elaborated on what he had told Pearl.

"Everything," he said. "Everything. Eggs, waffles, pancakes, cereal. Maggie and whoever else might have had ECT that morning would eat until the colored ladies shooed us out so they could clean the place for lunch. I sent her clothes home by Hubert as she outgrew them, and replaced them with shipments from Ellisberg's, all in graduated sizes, because we had no way of knowing how much larger she would become. She didn't go wild ordering the clothes over the phone. She just got some dresses she'd seen in the newspaper advertisements, pretty things, and stockings. No shoes. That was the first sign of real recovery. No new shoes. I asked her doctor about the weight gain, if it was good for her to be stuffing herself this way, and at every meal. He said it was fine. When she was depressed or manic, she simply did not eat. You know how thin she could get."

I remembered one manic summer when my mother was so thin that she filled the cavity between her collarbone and neck with water and walked around the yard with her arms outstretched, daring me to do the same and race her to the clothesline and back. She already had complete summer and winter wardrobes in sizes four up to eight, but never had I imagined she would let herself be seen in a ten.

She started acting like a member of the society of patients. Father said that she began having conversations with other people, that she did not cut them off or act preoccupied when they were speaking to her. She made friends. She talked with them about medication and release dates. She even let her roommate borrow her clothing. By way of Hubert, who acted as courier, she sent home crafts she made: a clay frog soap-holder, a hooked rug, a paint-by-number horse's head, a macramé wall hanging, a shoeshine box. These items accumulated on the Parsons bench in the front hall, and every time Pearl walked by she commented that she had to find a place for all that stuff.

"Your Aunt Menefee," Pearl told me, "will come in and hoot at this soap dish and this wall carpetry thing. If she comes by and pokes her head in to say woo-hoo, I suppose you could say you made everything at school. You tell her that."

Pearl was embarrassed for my mother, though she need not have been. I doubt that Mother felt ridiculous or even self-conscious as she sat at a long table with other women, sanding strips of wood, painting that frog bright green. Perhaps she remembered her creative arts award. Maybe she told the other patients about it. She probably felt she was accomplishing something, and that something had a beginning, a middle, and an end. That was the way life worked. Looking back, I see that she was practicing a new life Tuesdays through Sundays and was being shocked into normality on Mondays.

All of my days were taken with missing her terribly. I missed her face and her voice, and although I was not being shot through with an electrical current, I was, like my mother, barely capable of holding in my mind a crystalline memory. I could remember bits of unsynthesized information Freddy was feeding me, things like how the electoral college operated, how the Krebs cycle worked, the fact that the Puritans brushed their teeth with brimstone, butter, and gunpowder, but I had to squint at night in bed to remember my mother's face. I finally took a framed photograph from her bedroom and placed it on my dresser. I chose a picture that had been taken of us one winter day when I was a little more than a year old. My mother was pushing me in our family's old pram in downtown Rocky Mount, and when she stopped to look at a display of photographs in the window of Barringer's Studio, Mr. Barringer himself saw her and ran outside to ask if she would pose for an advertisement. For the next year, the picture ran in the newspaper over the caption "Stroll on by Barringer's!" In the photograph, I was sitting up, holding a rattle he had given me. My mother was smiling. She was not grinning maniacally. She was simply smiling.

One Sunday afternoon when Mother had been at Duke about a month, Hubert drove Freddy, Pearl, Olive, and me to visit her. Father was already there. He drove to see Mother on Friday evenings and stayed at the Blue Devil Lodge across the street from the hospital. He usually came home on Tuesday afternoons. My images of what I would see at Duke came straight from Dickens's descriptions of workhouses. Freddy would not tell me what to expect, and this may have been for the best, as his ideas probably came from Vincent Price movies. He slouched to the car. He slouched in the car. And he slouched all the way from the parking lot to the psychiatric ward, which looked like a place Mother would love. At first glance, it resembled the main, all-purpose room at Memorial Hospital, from *As the World Turns.* I wondered whether she had harangued any of the nurses about Dr. Bob Hughes, or Kim, or Penny, or Lisa, whether she had looked for them, or called people by their names. I wondered what she would look like, besides larger.

She was sitting on the side of her bed, which was covered with a lamb's-wool blanket Pearl had sent from home. When she got up to meet us, she hobbled forward like a grandmother with swollen ankles, headed for the door to greet out-of-town company. Because of fluid retention caused by all her medication, her legs looked as if they had been driven into her shoes, like pilings into a riverbed. Her hair had been cut and teased into a remarkable type of dome construction. I thought she looked inflated all over, like the Orphan Annie balloon in the Macy's Thanksgiving Day parade. The first thing she mentioned was her new hairstyle.

"Hey! Guess what?" she said. "The girl down the hall's a beautician. She did my hair! She's going to try something different as soon as her husband brings her magazines from the shop."

It is very difficult for a child to tell an enthusiastic mother that her hair looks awful, and so I was very glad when Pearl reached forth to embrace her. Mother hugged Freddy, who took his hands out of his pockets long enough to wrap his arms around her back, and then she came to me. I felt a mixture of wariness and eagerness. There was something about her, or maybe there was something about her being in that place, that gave me the heebie-jeebies and would not allow me to relax thoroughly when she enfolded me in her arms and told me it was good to see me. As much as I hungered for her, I felt like a puppy that has been scolded too many times for wetting the rug yet desperately wants the love and attention of its owner. I returned to Pearl, who put her arm around me and squeezed me hard on the shoulder. She must have noticed my tentative embrace. Then Mother started talking about how big Freddy and I were, even though we were both too old to have grown noticeably in a month. I remember thinking that she really needed something to say, that I had come all this way to see my mother and all we could think to say was how we'd grown. Without a rampage of Mother's in the air, we were foraging aimlessly for something to talk about.

Mr. Barnes had sent Mother a box of roses with us, but she wanted to wait until later to put them in water. His involvement with my mother's recovery was complicated by Miss Woodward, who started appearing less like a lonely old maid and more like a possessive lover. Before, he would have sent her robes and nightgowns, but once Miss Woodward began supervising the purchases, Mother received flowers, only flowers. As badly as he must have wanted to see Mother, he still would not visit Duke because of the unhappy associations hospitals had for him. But even if he had overcome his memory, I doubt he would have abided the other patients and their great boiling-over stew of sickness. He would have wanted them to snap out of their haze of barbiturate-induced insobriety, to buck up and act with more self-respect. It was quite beyond his ken to realize that showing self-respect and demonstrating self-restraint were two activities at the bottom of a sick person's list of things to do. He would have thought that if they had to be crazy, then they could do it in their rooms, not out in the dayroom during visiting hours. They could suffer off to the side, as Maggie had always done, or at least as she had until the day she drove off in the car.

A nurse came in and told Mother she would have to take her visitors to the dayroom. She could not remain in her room.

Mother told us she was still on watches. She said this pleasantly, in a whisper, the way a schoolgirl might lean forward over her desk and tell the girl in front of her, "I'm wearing a training brassiere today."

Father did not want Mother to discuss the number of days she had left on suicide watch, so he burst forth with questions about our schoolwork. Had we brought anything to show Mother?

Pearl had encouraged me to bring an essay on "The Celebrated Jumping Frog of Calaveras County," which Mother read and then hounded the other patients in the dayroom to read. She made them pass it around like a collection plate. She was well, I thought, but not *that* well. Pearl sat with her large pocketbook on her lap, and Olive did the same. Olive, however, looked around and was as curious as I was. Every now and then Pearl would tap Olive and me on the knee to make us stop staring at the other patients.

"You might draw one of them over to you, and then what are you going to do?" she whispered to Olive. "You came to see Miss Maggie. Stop looking."

Mother was trying to make Freddy talk. She was trying to energize him. I remember how badly his face was broken out, how he had cut himself trying to glide a razor over his pimples. Mother called attention to this as if they were alone in the bathroom at home. Father could not help us organize a conversation because he had started to deal with a man he had befriended who now wanted to make him chairman of the board of his company. I wondered whether the man meant what he said. Could Father make a lot more money? Could we move to New York? What sort of company did this man own? Mother, set firmly in the hospital's hierarchy of sanity, could not resist making him appear to be sicker than she ever had been.

"Mr. Boyd, tell my friend Pearl about your company," Mother said.

"Well, it's a greeting card outfit, you see. I'll be back in a jiff." He trotted down the hall.

Pearl huffed. " 'In a jiff.' What's he talking about?"

Father explained what the man had told him, that he saved all the cards he had received in the hospital, and he had the idea that he had manufactured them, that he owned his own large greeting card concern.

Mother beamed. "See? Now, that's when you're *really* sick. God, you do not know how much better I feel. I can't remember my name half the time, but oh boy, do I feel better."

Before the greeting card man could return, we went off for a little tour of the psychiatric unit, stopping only long enough for Mother to line up for her medications, the distribution of which seemed to be the main event of a patient's afternoon. She met the silvery cart as the nurse wheeled it out of the station, and other women came forward and put their hands on the top rim of the cart and ceremoniously walked it to the center of the room, like pallbearers. The little white paper cup full of pills looked to me like an old-fashioned nurse's cap. I can still see Mother tossing the pills into her mouth and swallowing water. Like the other patients, she had to open her mouth wide so the nurse could see if any pills were hidden underneath her tongue. Pearl asked Mother why people's mouths were inspected.

Mother told her that sometimes people were saving up pills and sometimes they were not in a hurry to get well. "It depends," she said, "on whether you're up or down. Some people like feeling too good, the way I used to."

"Yes, ma'am," Pearl told her, "and that's why you took off in the automobile."

Father gave Pearl a look that told her not to talk about Mother's old reality. She had a new reality, and it involved group therapy, psychoanalysis, arts and crafts, sing-alongs, Ping-Pong, and jigsaw puzzles. She showed us the bulletin board where all the week's events were posted and told us that one of these days she would be allowed to go to the movies and Friends of the College concerts that were available for patients who could be relied upon not to bolt. Being allowed to go on one of these trips was a new goal in her life. I remember how she put her hand by her mouth as though she did not want any of the staff to hear her disclosing shop secrets.

"Right now," she said, "they're scared I might get confused and run off. If I'm okay next week, they'll let me go with them to Van Cliburn."

I thought that if she was okay the next week then she could come home and start being a mother. Forget Van Cliburn, whoever he was. I wanted her back so that she could try out some of her fresh sanity on the family. She seemed to be having a good time in the hospital, and I wanted her to smear some of this happiness around.

Then we all walked to the cafeteria to have dinner. Freddy and I were not prepared for the spectacle of Mother at the table. She ate with her mouth open. She ate talking. She ate with her hands. My elegant mother licked chicken bones. We were all so busy monitoring our own reactions that nobody said a thing when Olive spoke into the air.

She said, "I'd stop her before she blows up."

When we walked Mother back to her room, we passed by the room of the greeting card man. The door was open. He was sitting on his bed with his cards splayed out in front of him, as if he were playing a game of solitaire. I remember the way Pearl put two fingers up to her mouth, telling me to be extra quiet so he would not notice us. Father had gotten permission for Mother to walk us to the public waiting room, as long as he walked her back, but she told him she would stay on the ward.

"Thank you for the offer," she said, "but I would prefer not to."

The response sounded like something she had learned how to say in the hospital, a phrase her doctor had planted in her brain when he was installing a new personality. I left the hospital sad. My feelings centered on her new hairdo, being right there on her head in such proximity to her brain. Perhaps the new style was an indicator, like a weather vane, oriented to show us that she would come home changed, maybe bland, cut and teased like other women. Pearl had Hubert stop at a Dairy Queen on the way home. My brother would not order anything. He just slouched toward Rocky Mount.

Fifteen

Waiting for Mother's arrival back home was like what it must have been for a mourner standing on the edge of the tracks watching for the train carrying the body of Lincoln or Franklin Roosevelt to pass. Even though it was cold, I sat on the front porch steps and waited, thinking every now and then how much more my father had to drive from Durham, wondering whether Mother's head would still be large, her ankles still swollen, and the new fat around her middle bouncy and jiggly. I had no clear picture of who it was I was expecting, except my mother, and this meant little more to me than waiting for one of the personalities in her collection to walk through the door. Would I see her, really see her? Like that waiting mourner beside the tracks, I hoped I might catch a glimpse behind the curtains.

Mr. Barnes and Miss Woodward were there with us, along with Aunt Menefee and Uncle Lawrence. They were inside the house. I had moved over to let them walk up the steps past me, and only Uncle Lawrence and Miss Woodward greeted me. Mr. Barnes had been saying something about Martin Luther King, Jr., whom he considered a Communist. Going in the door, Aunt Menefee remarked that King did not know his place—a complaint I had sometimes heard her make to Father about Pearl. Aunt Menefee had left her children at home because they had preferred to watch television. Freddy was shut up in his room. I knew he would avoid Mr. Barnes as long as he could. He would emerge from his room to greet Mother and have dinner, and then he would retreat.

Miss Woodward had brought a turkey and some vegetables in the trunk of Mr. Barnes's car, and Pearl and Olive were in the kitchen reheating everything. Hubert had disappeared, as he was apt to do whenever any change was taking place in the household. He had been gone for days in Pearl's car, which had last been seen outside a place called Wright's Chick Shack. His act nearly spoiled the good humor Pearl felt over Mother's homecoming. She implored my father to fire Hubert when he was found. "Or I might do it myself," she said. She was so mad she called a sheriff's deputy, who came and made her even hotter when he told my father, within her range of hearing, that he would not pursue Hubert because he did not want to get involved in a "nigra mess."

When I saw Father's car coming down the road, I ran into the house and shouted that Mother was on the way. Everyone came out onto the porch and waited. When the car came in the driveway, Mr. Barnes was the first to go down the steps to meet it. The rest of us followed. Freddy stood by Olive in his Steve McQueen outfit of a sweatshirt and putty-colored jeans and worked at avoiding Mr. Barnes's glances, which seemed to say, "Act right when your mother gets out of that goddamn car."

Mother's feet were on the ground almost before Father stopped the car. She was still large, but when Mr. Barnes offered a hand to help her, she hopped out as though she were a twig of a woman. She embraced Mr. Barnes and then Miss Woodward, who had walked up be-

side him. Then she turned to us. She did not
lumber. Her step was sprightly. We had
formed a ragged receiving line, beginning
with Mr. Barnes and ending with Olive. Pearl
moved me in front of herself and stood with
her hands on my shoulders, and when Mother
got to me, Pearl gave me a little shove toward
her. Mother put her arms around me and
lifted me off the ground. Mr. Barnes warned
her not to put her back out. She told him not
to worry. I thought he was jealous because she
had not treated him as effusively.

"We have so much to do," she whispered
in my ear.

I assumed she meant that we would do
everything we had never done. I wanted to
ask, "Like what, exactly?" but the question
seemed inappropriate. Knowing that she was
coming home well and therefore with no excuse not to be my mother, I had accumulated
a list of things she and I could do together. I
wanted her to sit on the edge of my bed at
night and talk to me the way June Cleaver
sometimes talked to Beaver. I wanted her to
cook something, anything, and let me help
her. She, and not Pearl, could rustle me out of
bed in the mornings. She could fix my hair in
a French braid, something Olive did for me,
although she called the braid a "big cornrow."

The list went on and on. But instead of telling her that I also knew we had a big agenda, I merely thanked her and let her set me back on the ground.

Pearl was next. I heard Mother thank her for looking after Freddy and me in her absence. Pearl could have told her that she had been gone a lot longer than eight weeks, but she did not. She told Mother that we had been "the best chirrun." Then Mother hugged Freddy, said something that I could not hear, and walked toward the house with her arm around his waist. I noticed the way she strolled, neither too fast nor too slow. She was wearing a camel-hair coat, not the red swing coat that had gotten her into so much trouble. I was glad to see her hair in a bun instead of that dome. I liked the way it was loosely done, poufing out. I thought she was gorgeous, her skin no longer in danger of becoming like that of the crones at church. As she passed Olive, she reached out and squeezed her hand, thanking her for tending to the house while she was away. Again, somebody could have told Mother that, figuratively speaking, she had been at home only rarely since the place was built, but we would not have dared spoil a second of her arrival.

Mother told me to come into the kitchen

with her and help finish putting the food out.
This was new. Mother had never helped Pearl
in the kitchen. The day she sat on the floor
with the cookbooks around her, looking for
what Catholics ate, was probably the last time
she was involved with preparing a meal. Father kept telling her she should lie down and
take a rest before she started any chores, but
she would not hear of a nap.

"I know perfectly well what I am and am
not capable of," she said. "It's not as if I've
offered to go run in a footrace. I just want to
help with lunch."

When we got to the kitchen, it was evident
that everything had already been done. But
Mother insisted on doing something anyway,
so Pearl gave her my job, a child's task of putting ice in glasses.

Soon after we were all seated at the table,
Mr. Barnes and Father announced that they
wanted to hire Mother to keep books for their
rental property. She said she was flattered by
the offer, and agreed to take it. I was afraid
for her. I thought she might still be too wobbly
to take on that responsibility. I had never
considered my mother a worker. Father, I
thought, would have to keep her straightened
out.

Meanwhile, she had her own announcements to make. She wanted to declare the way things needed to be in the household for her to stay well. She had been making declarations my whole life, but this time she was not yelling them. She spoke in a deliberate way. Chiefly, she did not want any "sudden upsets." She needed a routine, she said, not unlike the one she had had in the hospital, and it was up to everyone in the family to let her know plans in advance, so she could ready herself. She told us she had always felt like Lucy the time she and Ethel were wrapping candies at a conveyor belt which moved along faster than they could work. Checking on them, their boss somehow did not realize that they were stuffing candies in their pockets, hats, mouths, in order to give the appearance that all was going well. The boss, gratified by their efficiency, yelled, "Let 'er roll!" and the belt moved faster and faster. Lucy and Ethel became frantic, and at the end of the day their stomachs hurt and they had to admit failure to Ricky and Fred.

"Now that I'm home," she said, "I don't want more candy than I can manage. Okay?"

She continued to say that if I had an event during the school year, she wanted it marked on the calendar. If Father had a dinner meeting with the Junior Order, that must be marked as well. If Mr. Barnes wanted to ride horses with her, he could no longer just show up and expect her to pull on a pair of boots. She might be busy. He could call and make plans with her. She had no decrees for Miss Woodward or for Uncle Lawrence and Aunt Menefee, although she looked at them hard, as though she was trying to come up with some.

Mr. Barnes was the only one at the table who chuckled at Mother's new assertiveness. The rest of us were a bit bewildered by her, even Father. Apparently she had not spoken with him about her plans on the way home. The place, I thought, would be like a friendly military camp. Pearl's role was being whittled back now that Mother was here, and Olive would be no more than a chambermaid. Mother announced that she was going to cook two nights a week, starting as soon as she created a recipe file from her cookbooks. She wanted her sewing machine taken out of the attic and oiled because she intended to make some of my clothes for me. Also, she wanted a driver's license. She meant to take me off a school bus full of hooligans who had always yelled out the windows and awakened her in the afternoons, and drive me to and from school herself. I was impressed, and I wondered if she had spent her last days in the hospital filling out a list of things to do.

Father's response was a comprehensive "I don't see why not," to all her requests.

I had recently watched *Invasion of the Body Snatchers* on a Saturday Monster Matinee. My mother, I thought, was like a pod person, so level, almost flat, yet clipping along at this recently programmed pace. I knew her by her highs and lows, and now, with these ends lopped off, she was right in the middle of her spectrum. She sounded kind without being cloying, brisk without being abrupt, forthright without being aggressive. She meant to be part of humanity, and we were not going to stop her.

Before Pearl started serving the food, Mother asked Freddy to say grace, something we never did except on Thanksgiving and Christmas. I cringed when he started the "God is great" prayer. That was all he knew. Although we knew Mr. Barnes did not approve of this childish, jingly prayer, neither of us had heard Father's "Bless us, our Heavenly Father" prayer enough to memorize it. Mr. Barnes glowered at Freddy when we raised our eyes.

Mother saw what was happening and diverted Mr. Barnes's attention. She asked what had ever become of old Mr. Tucker, a man with eleven children, who, during the Depression, hung a sign over his table that read: "Those that eat here, work here. No bums allowed." He had been a friend of Mr. Barnes's. This fact did not surprise me. Mr. Barnes told Mother that the man had died of a heart attack in his tobacco barn, with many of his children around him.

"And I bet they rushed right over to help him." Mother laughed at her joke.

"No, they did not," Mr. Barnes said. "They treated him like a cur dog. Didn't send for the doctor until it was too late."

Miss Woodward and Mother agreed that Mr. Tucker had been repaid in his own coinage, but Aunt Menefee, eager as always to gain Mr. Barnes's favor, said it was a shame for a father to be treated that way. I looked at Freddy and saw him smiling discreetly into his plate. Later he told me he had been imagining Mr. Barnes in a fit of unrelieved choking. Everyone made small talk while Pearl served the food, and when she was through, Miss Woodward called her to her chair and whispered into her ear.

Pearl shouted, "Ooo Lord! I have left it in the oven!" She trotted off to the kitchen and returned soon afterward with oyster dressing piled high in a serving dish. She started with Miss Woodward and proceeded around the table, apologizing all the while for the tardiness of the dressing. When she got to me, I told her, "No, thank you," and when she got to Freddy he told her the same.

Mr. Barnes put his fork down. "Something wrong with the food?" he asked us.

Not wanting to hear what she sensed was coming, Pearl set the dish on the table and disappeared into the kitchen.

Mother told Mr. Barnes that everything was delicious, and she thanked Miss Woodward for bringing the meal.

But he would not let it go. "What I mean to say," he told us, "is that when I was a boy, you ate what was on the table."

"Well, that's grand," Mother sighed, "but Freddy and Hattie don't like oyster dressing. I think you have to develop a taste for it. They've taken plenty of everything else."

Miss Woodward did not seem to mind that we were shunning her dressing, but she did not speak up. Mr. Barnes continued. "I think they're both coddled," he told my parents.

What a surprising remark, I thought, coming from someone who had always spoiled my mother. Father tried to say that the turkey was especially moist, but Mr. Barnes stopped him mid-sentence and spoke to Freddy. "What I want to know is what you're going to do when you get off to college and don't have a nigger cook to cater for you."

Mother folded her napkin in her lap. She seemed to be through eating. "Pearl is not the so-called nigger cook," she told him. "She's part of this family, and I'll not have anybody, including you, talk about her that way."

Mr. Barnes tried to back-pedal. "All I meant to say was, when Freddy gets to college he might not be able to be so choicey about what he eats."

Freddy mumbled, "They have a cafeteria line."

"See?" Mother said. "He can be as choicey as he wants to be, and when Hattie goes to school she stands in a line and chooses what she wants to eat also. I've been to the school. I know it. Now, I want this to stop."

Mr. Barnes smiled at her, or rather, he smirked.

"I don't see anything funny," she told him. "You just can't auger in on the children because they won't eat a serving of oyster dressing. Now, I mean it."

Mr. Barnes's hands were on either side of his plate. He looked as though he might swiftly hurl it across the room. Miss Woodward put a hand on top of his. He needed calming. I doubt that anybody, except perhaps his father, had ever talked to him that way. He moved himself back from the table and told Miss Woodward they were leaving. She stood with him, and they both turned and left the dining room and went straight out toward the front door. When Mother was unwell, I had seen her run Aunt Menefee off from the house, but here she was well, turning Mr. Barnes away and not getting up to chase him, to beg him to return to the table, where all would be well.

Father waited until he heard the door shut before he asked Mother if she was okay. So much for no "sudden upsets," I thought.

She told him she was fine. "I'll just not have that kind of behavior," she said.

She seemed proud to have won such a considerable victory so soon after her return. At first, we did not know what to say to her. Not even Father. And then Freddy looked up from the plate he was hunched over, gazed at Mother, and said, "Wow."

"And I," Mother told Freddy, "haven't had my noon nerve pills yet." I knew from overhearing Father talking to Pearl that one of the drugs she was coming home on was called Miltown. The name intrigued me, causing me to think of the hosiery mill on the other side of Rocky Mount, rackety looms, and streets lined with shotgun shacks for the workers.

I really liked my mother right then, as unfamiliar as she still was to me. I was sure that Mr. Barnes liked her, too, but I believed he was mad that she was so well. I knew he was going to miss her. Nothing could take her place with him, not even Miss Woodward with her perfect pies and casseroles. My mother had always been his clinging vine, and now she had grown arms, found shears, and cut herself off at the root. She was her own now, not his, and all over a catalytic plate of oyster dressing.

After Mother and I helped Olive clear the table, I went to my room to read. On the way upstairs I heard Mother telling Father, "It's naptime."

"Let me help you," he said.

"I can manage," she responded. I heard the smack of their kissing, and then he told her to sleep well.

I was in my room just a few minutes when she called my name. She shouted for me to come to her room. "And bring a book!" she said.

I went to her room, carrying *Frankenstein*. She was waiting at the open door. "Come in and let's read," she said. I was too astounded to stand there and enjoy any rush of exuberance over hearing her command. She walked over, sat on the edge of her bed, and started taking the pins out of her hair.

"Crawl in," she said.

Going around to my father's side of the bed, I studied her. All her hairpins were now in a ceramic dish on her nightstand, and she was lifting the front of her skirt, unhooking her stocking from her garter. I wondered how much farther she was going to go. Would she undress into a shift? Would I see her in her brassiere? I lay on the bed and turned my back to her, hoping she would hurry and tell me what was happening. I was most afraid of her announcing that we were about to have a long talk, the one I thought I had always wanted. It appeared, though, that she had brought me in only to read with her, so that is what I started doing. When she was through with her stockings, she went to one of her suitcases and took out a copy of *East of Eden*. She came back to the bed, fluffed her pillows, and lay down.

"This book has too many people in it," she said, "but I'm committed to it now."

I saw stamped on the edges of the pages "Property of Duke University Medical Center." I asked if they had let her take the book.

I worried about her having stolen it.

"No, they didn't," she said. "Do you know what my bill was?"

The question did not seem to require an answer.

"Let's read and go to sleep and then wake up and let your father take us to town. I just want to see things," she said.

She opened the book and read, and in a few minutes she was asleep. She had not said that she was sorry for the past years, and she had not promised that the future would always be different. I do not know what I would have done if she had launched into a tender moment. Maybe I would have told her, in my child's language, that the past did not matter. All that mattered was that she was by me, apparently strong and well and whole. That was good enough for the time being.

I fell asleep to the sound of Pearl's singing as she washed dishes. Mother must have woken before I did and placed a quilt over me, and then Father shook me awake late in the afternoon and said we were going to town. I remember hoping, very simply, that Mother would take me into a store and buy me something new to wear. Pearl had always given me great freedom when we went shopping, letting me choose what I thought suitable, and then handing the cashier a check signed by my father and a well-worn note which read, "Please let Miss Pearl Wiggins write this check against my account." Now I wanted Mother to choose something for me. I was eager to see what she would select.

We went to Belk's, Mother's favorite department store. First we walked to the young men's section, though Freddy swore he did not need anything. But Mother seemed intent on buying him something. He finally chose a blue flannel jacket and gray slacks. Father kept asking Mother if she thought she should be out and about. Shouldn't she be back at home, taking things easy?

"I want to do this, and I'm going to do this," she told him.

Next we went to my department, where she bought me a red boiled-wool coat with a matching hat and muff. One of my Madame Alexander dolls had a muff. I was thrilled. Mother told us we would all start going to church every Sunday because I would have somewhere to wear my coat. She asked Father if he needed anything, and he said he did not. She bought nothing for herself. On the way out of the store, Father stopped at the perfume counter and made her accept a bottle of White Shoulders.

That night, after we got home, Mother came into my room while I was in bed reading. She entered without knocking. I worried again that the long-awaited mother-daughter talk was about to occur. I braced myself as she walked over to the bed and sat down beside me.

"Do you like your new coat?" she asked.

I told her I did, and then she told me I could show it off at school the following Monday as long as I promised not to get it dirty. Looking back, I believe she was as nervous as I was, grateful that a new coat gave us something concrete to fix on. But that night, she seemed thoroughly in control, self-assured. She looked all around my room, and then she got up and went to the cork bulletin board and peered at my friends' school pictures in the half-light. Then she walked over to my shelf of dolls and touched several of their dresses.

When she came back to sit on the bed, all she said was, "Well, don't stay up too late." I told her I would go right to sleep. I was eager to obey her, happy to have received motherly instruction from her. After she left the room and I turned out the light on my nightstand, I still felt her presence, her wholly satisfactory presence. A torrent of apology, of words, had not been necessary for me to know that she loved me. I could tell by the way she lingered in the doorway, reluctant to leave.

Mother woke up every morning and dressed as though she were going to a job in town. She had Pearl drive her around first thing to collect rents that were due. The tenants paid by the week. Then she drank coffee and gave Pearl her orders for the day. Then she listened to *Ask Your Neighbor* on the radio and worked on needlepointing monogrammed pillows. After I did my homework each day, she let me practice until I got the knack, saying nothing when she had to take out my backward stitches. In the evenings, Mother worked on Mr. Barnes's and Father's bookkeeping at the kitchen table. She would spread out the green ledger sheets in front of her and ask not to be bothered until she finished.

She had Father pick up a guide for her driving test, and she studied safety rules and practiced three-point turns between the deep ditches on either side of the path to Mr. Barnes's house. She parallel-parked between my father's car and Pearl's. Hubert had finally been found with her car, after Pearl suggested some places to look and sent Father in search of him, saying no "clean" woman should set foot in any of the houses he was liable to be visiting. When Father spotted the car, it was parked in a front yard with ten others, all of them, including Pearl's, up on blocks. Hubert had lent a friend the tires so he could drive to Baltimore. Father had to buy more tires, put them on, and have them balanced before he could come home, with Hubert driving behind him.

Father tuned up Mother's sewing machine, and together she and I went to the fabric store and bought material for spring clothes that she could sew throughout the winter. She let me sit close by her as we looked through all the pattern books, and we reached agreements about what I wanted and what she had the skills to sew. The patterns we came out of the store with were for very simple outfits, not unlike what little Amish girls might wear if they could play in shorts, but I did not mind. My mother was making them for me. When we got home, she went to work right away, cutting, pinning, basting. I stood still and let her measure me all over.

Mother fought confusion and would not let herself be drawn into a conversation that promised any shade of gray as its resolution. She talked a great deal about the weather. It was all wrong. She said that she had missed

the fall colors entirely and that this had mud-
dled her brain more than the illness had. The
way she dealt with it, she said, was to move
on to winter and forget that autumn had ever
occurred. She wanted the season to pass in a
hurry, and then maybe she would feel caught
up. She said it was as bad as when she lived
in Louisiana and enjoyed the onset of spring
there, banks of azaleas in full blossom, and
then came up to North Carolina and went
through it all again, starting with a lone crocus
in the yard. Most people would love two
springs, but for a person like my mother,
whose interior rhythms were unruly, having
two of the same season or missing one entirely
was disorienting.

Initially, I might have been puzzled by
Mother's reentry, by the apparent disappear-
ance of her extremes of depression and exul-
tation, but Father was grateful for the respite.
Even then, however, her presence took time to
sink in, to soak into his dreams.

"When she was home from the hospital," he
once told me, "I would still have the same
dream. I had the dream for months, the very
one I had before she was hospitalized. It's five
or six o'clock in the morning, and I hear all
our migrant laborers at the front door. I go
outside to see what's happening, and there she

lies at the foot of the steps. They've pulled her out of the irrigation pond and brought her to me and just dropped her body there the way a cat deposits a mouse. She's wearing her white eyelet robe, and I can see the pockets still full of rocks she's weighted herself down with. The Mexicans are babbling about quitting because of the bad luck, and then Pearl comes running, and then you, and then Freddy. I don't know what to do. I'm hung. I don't know whether to try to revive her, she looks so gone, or send you back in the house, or call Father, or what. I end up firing all the Mexicans on the spot, and then your mother opens her eyes and her mouth and says, "Now, that was a fine thing to do. Who's going to pick all those cucumbers?" And then she closes her eyes again."

Mother continued going about her life as she had announced she would. She kept appearing at my door at night, telling me not to stay up so late reading, not to fall asleep with the light on. She drove me to school each morning, but she did not kiss me when I got out of the car. It seemed as though she was coming only part of the way to me. I wondered what she was waiting for, what was holding her back from joining me entirely. It did not occur to me at the time that she knew as little about being my mother as I knew about being her daughter. I could have leaned over in the car for a kiss or asked her to come tuck me in bed nights, but I did not. I could have offered her an open path toward me, but instead, I waited for her. Maybe, I thought, she would come to me when she was all-the-way well, a condition her doctor told Father would take months to settle in, to sustain itself.

We would both have to become accustomed to each other. Every day we had missed being together was a day we had to make up. She had to do the same work with Freddy, although the job was made more difficult by his absence at college and then medical school. But they managed. After he left, she would write him early in the mornings and ask me to put the letters in the mailbox before we left for school. The envelopes were always fat. He wrote her every few days, and when he came home on vacations, he helped her in the garden, and followed her around the kitchen while she and Pearl canned vegetables, reaching high places for them on the pantry shelves. He remained as fascinated by her as I was. And when Father was at home, mooning over her, she fairly had to step over him to go about her day.

She stayed sane thanks to ample medication, particularly Miltown and then lithium carbonate, psychotherapy, and sheer dint of will. She never decided that the state of mania had felt good enough for a return visit. There was never any more havoc, never any more terror in our house. Every day she tried to be well, the earnest way a child will try to be good on the days before Christmas. Only, Mother was uniformly successful. She was present at the events of my life, small and large, from normal, quiet mornings in the kitchen with Pearl, to her surprise appearance at the back of the auditorium the day I was inducted into the honor society. We never sat down and had a long, constructive and restorative talk, but that mattered less and less to me as I grew older. Her actions were more important. Maybe she could not have borne to dredge up the past and its pain. Maybe I could not have, either. We were somehow able to get at the business of living without calling up ghosts. We let the past stay in the past.

Until I sat down to conjure her memory, I had forgotten the worry and the wounds of my childhood. In remembering her now, I have remembered also the pain her illness caused me and my inexplicable joy at her return to me. Both forgiving and healing are true arts, and in telling my mother's story I have been able to forgive the past without reservation and heal myself without concern over a lapse into acute sorrow over her death. I now understand the miracle of catharsis, the value of her story. I see her leaning on a rake she has been using on a carpet of yellow and gold leaves in the front yard, watching me, saying nothing, just smiling. I am across the yard, fifteen years old, helping Hubert mound leaves into a wheelbarrow that he will cart off to the edge of the woods behind our house. I stop to smile back at her, and I can still feel the warmth of the autumn sun and her gaze. I also see her, finally, poised to fall from those steps years later, so well for so long, and not ready to die. Although I am forced to see her startled, tumbling, it is her other, peaceful and smiling face that is fixed in my mind: always the indelible memory of her face in the clear, infinite light of October.

AVON BOOKS TRADE PAPERBACKS

MEMOIR FROM ANTPROOF CASE   72733-1/$14.00 US/$19.00 Can
    by Mark Heplrin

A SOLDIER OF THE GREAT WAR   72736-6/$15.00 US/$20.00 Can
    by Mark Heplrin

THE LONGEST MEMORY   72700-5/$10.00 US
    by Fred D'Aguiar

COCONUTS FOR THE SAINT   72630-0/$11.00 US/$15.00 Can
    by Debra Spark

WOMEN AND GHOSTS   72501-0/$9.00 US/$12.00 Can
    by Alison Lurie

BRAZZAVILLE BEACH   78049-6/$11.00 US
    by William Boyd

COYOTE BLUE   72523-1/$12.00 US/$16.00 Can
    by Christopher Moore

TASTING LIFE TWICE: LITERARY   78123-9/$12.00 US/$16.00 Can
LESBIAN FICTION BY NEW
AMERICAN WRITERS
    Edited by E. J. Levy

CHARMS FOR THE EASY LIFE   72557-6/$12.00 US/$16.00 Can
    by Kaye Gibbons

THE MEN AND THE GIRLS   72408-1/$10.00 US
    by Joanna Trollope

THE LEGEND OF BAGGER VANCE   72751-X/$12.00 US/$16.00 Can
    by Steven Pressfield